NET ASSETS

by

JENNIFER JANE POPE

CHIMERA

Net Asset first published in 1998 by
Chimera Publishing Ltd
PO Box 152
Waterlooville
Hants
PO8 9FS

Printed and bound in Great Britain by
Caledonian International Book Manufacturing Ltd
Glasgow

New authors welcome

NET ASSET

Jennifer Jane Pope

CHAPTER ONE

Lianne stared at her reflection in the tall mirror and swallowed nervously. It had taken five vodkas to come this far – five vodkas and an hour and a half in a haze of talcum powder, makeup, hairspray and rubber. Mostly rubber it seemed; looking, discussing, deciding, and finally, fitting. Squeezing legs and arms, feet and hands, breasts, stomach, and thighs into the clinging latex. Forcing feet and toes into the ridiculously high heeled ankle boots and tottering unsteadily across the carpet, fighting for balance, convinced she must fall headlong and break an ankle – or worse.

Now, slightly more sober than when she and Ellen had first arrived, Lianne was beginning to have second thoughts. She could not believe that the person staring back at her was herself. Lianne Connolly was the typical girl next door; worked as a receptionist at the Health Centre, wore her blonde hair in a neat pony tail, did her weekly shopping at the supermarket, and drove a five year old Metro into town to buy her conservative clothes. Lianne Connolly did not wear rubber corsets, stockings and gloves, perch on four inch heels and wear latex knickers so thin and stretched that you could see every detail of her sex as plainly as if it were naked.

She turned away and stumbled back towards the bed and her handbag, needing the packet of cigarettes that had lain forgotten inside it since the day, three weeks before, when she had taken the decision to quit. That was the day after the hatchet-faced administrator at work had told her she was being made redundant, and two days before she had first met Ellen Sanderson. Her rubber-sheathed fingers fumbled with the packet, tearing the cardboard in her haste to get it open. Picking out a cigarette was no easy matter with the unfamiliar latex desensitising her usually nimble fingers, and retrieving the lighter from the muddled depths of the bag was a further challenge. Eventually she felt it nestling in a bottom corner, took it out and flicked it into flame at the fourth attempt. Her hands were trembling so badly now that it took a supreme effort of concentration to bring the flame to the tip of the cigarette, but she finally managed it and greedily sucked in the foul-tasting smoke. She exhaled slowly, marvelling at how bad it tasted after even such a short lay-off and wondering, more importantly, just what she was going to do.

It had seemed easy enough when Ellen had suggested it. Cash in the hand, a week's work – maybe more – and no real effort required.

'It's just modelling, sweetie,' Ellen had reassured her. 'We dress up, some bloke takes our pictures and then this artist chap produces drawings from the prints. Easy, don't you reckon?' Lianne had expressed her doubts.

'But rubber and leather?' she had said, uncertainly. 'It seems a bit, well, you know, over the top.'

'Listen, hon,' Ellen had persisted, gripping her hand between her own, 'if I'd said it was modelling cardigans and slacks you'd have jumped at it for two hundred quid a day. The problem is, the twin sets and catalogue market is all tied up and they mostly don't pay that sort of money. And they don't let you keep a couple of outfits as a bonus.'

'I don't think I'd want a rubber outfit, bonus or otherwise,' Lianne had laughed nervously. Ellen had not given up.

'Look, Lianne,' she urged, 'you need the money. You're out of work and there aren't that many jobs around here, unless you fancy being a shop girl or a shelf stacker. That piddling pittance they gave you as redundancy pay is just about gone, isn't it, even with what I pay towards the rent of this place. You can't afford to turn down a chance like this.'

'If it's that good, why don't they use experienced models?' Lianne had challenged her new flatmate.

'They do,' Ellen assured her, 'but when this Stacey girl was whipped off to have her appendix sorted, I thought of you. I told George and Nadia I had the ideal stand-in. I even told them you'd done a bit of basic stuff whilst you were at school.'

'But they'll know that's a lie the moment they see me,' Lianne protested. Ellen laughed.

'Why should they? Look, you're a pretty blonde, even if you don't make much of yourself most of the time. You've got nice legs, a cute bum, and great tits. All you need to do is walk right and stand right, and in some of those boots and corsets you can't do anything but, believe me. Come on, Lianne, don't be a scaredy-cat!'

In the end, the combination of Ellen's cajolery and the lure of between fifteen hundred and two thousand pounds cash proved too much for Lianne and she had agreed to go along with her new friend.

Now, perched on the edge of the bed, encased in shining rubber, it didn't seem quite so simple. She should have realised it from the moment they had first pulled up the driveway and parked outside the imposing entrance, to be greeted by a woman clad in polished knee high boots, shining black leather miniskirt and leather waistcoat over a pure white, silk blouse. Nadia Muirhead, Editor-in-Chief of Darius Publishing Ltd, looked as though she might have just walked off the cover of one of the glossy magazines that adorned the top shelf of the little Asian newsagency just down the road from Lianne's flat. Not that she had ever studied those publications too closely, but it was hard to miss them, even if they were displayed twelve inches above head height.

In her early forties, with her bright green eyes and her jet-black hair swept up into an elegant chignon, Nadia would have made an imposing figure even without her leather couture. Lianne estimated that she would have stood five feet ten in her black stockinged feet and the extra five inches provided by the heels of her boots were totally over the top, in her opinion.

'Thank you so much for jumping into the breech at such short notice,' she greeted Lianne, proffering a hand on which every finger glittered with gold and precious stones. Her grip was firm, like a man's, Lianne had noticed and had been relieved to retrieve her own fingers still in one piece. 'I'll leave Ellen to show you the way,' Nadia continued. 'First shoot is in two hours, most of which you'll need to get into costume, etcetera, but I expect you already know about that. Suzy'll be free in about fifteen minutes and I'll send her up to you then.'

The house, which was early nineteenth century, was an impressive piece of architecture with two protruding wings and three storeys, above which dormer windows poked their noses from a massive tiled roof.

Ellen led the way into an entrance hall that was large enough to hold a tennis court, and up a wide staircase that was pure Jane Austen. Between the first and second floors the stairway was far narrower, but Lianne calculated there would still have been enough room to drive her car up it, such was the scale on which the entire place had been built.

Their room was on the second floor at the eastern end of the house; a bedroom which would have swallowed Lianne's entire flat whole. The furniture appeared to be from the same period as the house, for no one in their right mind would try to get wardrobes and chests that size into a modern semi. The bedstead was brass and could have slept three with elbowroom to spare, but Lianne guessed that the owners of this house would never be that pushed for accommodation. As Ellen closed the door, Lianne just stood in the centre of the pale pink carpet and stared, both at the room itself and at the panoramic view of the Sussex Downs that the huge window afforded.

'Our stuff is in there,' Ellen said, indicating the larger of the two wardrobes. 'It'll be freshly washed and powdered, all ready for us.'

'Powdered?' Lianne asked, slightly nonplussed. Ellen grinned.

'Talcum powder,' she explained. 'Getting into latex is a bitch without it, believe me. Come on, get stripped off and I'll show you. Suzy will be up in a minute and we've got less time than you think.'

The two girls stripped off together. Ellen seemed quite at ease with the exercise, but Lianne, who had never been naked with another girl since the schooldays shower room, was less relaxed about it. She knew she had a nice body, for Colin had never tired of telling her so. But then Colin had finally dumped her for that stick-insect creature with the mile long legs who had started working Friday nights behind the bar down at *The Stag*, and Lianne had realised, too late, that he would compliment any female he thought would lay still long enough for him. Having said that, Lianne realised that having a 36-24-36 figure was something a lot of girls envied her for, especially as her boobs filled a C-cup comfortably and her legs were long and shapely.

Ellen, at five feet eight inches, was two inches the taller, her bust an impressive 38D. She was an inch or so broader about the hips too, and her firm buttocks jutted out in the most provocative fashion. Her blue eyes were greyer than Lianne's, and her face, though longer and leaner, was just as attractive. Between them the two young women made an attractive sight as they finally stood naked on the soft carpet.

'Let's get you dressed first,' Ellen suggested. 'You're playing the part of Marylou, my girl Friday. My character is Della de Linkwent, rogue private investigator.'

'Sounds a bit daft to me,' Lianne mumbled. Ellen winked at her.

'It is all a bit daft,' she said. 'It's a comic strip adventure, after all. Look, I thought I'd already explained. Della and Marylou go in search of a missing heiress, who's been kidnapped by the mysterious Madame B and her band of merry men and girls. Naturally, everything goes wrong and the two of them – the two of us – also fall into the clutches of the villains. The story-line's a bit thin, but the main thing is that our two heroines get to dress in all the kinky gear and get into all sorts of awkward positions, if you know what I mean.'

Lianne was not sure she did know what Ellen meant, but she decided to say nothing. She rummaged in her handbag and brought out the remains of the small bottle, unscrewing the cap and tipping the burning contents straight down her throat. As she coughed and wiped the tears from her eyes, Ellen grinned.

'Bit of Dutch courage?' she said. 'No harm in that.'

'Why do you think I had those two doubles when we stopped at the pub?' Lianne replied, dropping the empty bottle back from where it had come. Ellen stared at her, aghast.

'Doubles?' she squeaked. 'I thought they were singles. I'd never have let you drive if I'd known.'

'Well, it's too late now,' Lianne snapped. 'If I hadn't had them then, I'd have turned back. I'm nervous as hell, in case you hadn't noticed.'

'Just relax,' Ellen urged her. 'There really is nothing to it.'

When Ellen started fastening the rubber corset about her waist, however, Lianne was not sure at all. The garment was thick and tough, fastening at the front with a series of businesslike looking steel clasps. It reached to the top of her thighs, dipping a little at the front, but high at the back to leave her buttocks exposed. There were three-quarter cup supports at the top that lifted Lianne's breasts dramatically, giving her a far deeper cleavage than she had ever had before, and this was emphasised by the way the corset pinched her waist in by at least two inches. However, two inches was not to be the limit, as she discovered when Ellen turned her attention to the laces at the back and began steadily drawing them in.

'I can't breathe!' Lianne protested, holding onto the foot of the bed for support. 'You can't get it any tighter than it already is.' Behind her, Ellen grunted and puffed.

'Don't you believe it,' she retorted. 'Just breathe shallowly and I'll get this closed if it's the last thing I do.'

'It'll probably be the last thing I ever do, you mean,' Lianne gasped, but Ellen was as good as her word and, when she finally knotted off the thick cords, Lianne was the proud, though highly dubious, owner of an impossibly cinched waist. She stood there, red-faced, staring at her new contours in the mirror.

'What do you think?' Ellen asked. 'Really sexy shape, isn't it?'

'Really drastic is more like it,' Lianne sulked. 'How long do I have to endure this torture?'

'Only for a few hours,' Ellen replied airily. 'You'll soon get used to it, anyway.' Lianne doubted that she would, but consoled herself with the thought of the fee she was earning. And nothing could be worse than facing the line of sniffling kids, mums, and pensioners that she had endured during her three years at the Health Centre.

After the corset came the stockings, which were made of a much thinner fabric. Ellen showed Lianne how to roll them down and ease her foot into the bottom of the powdered tube, coaxing the latex over her toes and heel until it fit snugly about her ankle. Then it was a matter of persuading the rubber up over her knee, smoothing it out so that it hugged her calf, and then finally rolling it up her thigh and fastening it to the bottom of the corset with the three sturdy rubber suspender straps. The stockings were long, reaching right up into the crease between thigh and groin and, when the second one was finally in place, Lianne's legs looked as though they had been sprayed with a new skin.

The panties were cut high on the thigh and plunged low at the front, barely covering her pubic hair, the gossamer latex molding itself to the contours of Lianne's sex and leaving nothing to the imagination. She hoped the skirt, or dress, would at least be long enough to cover her modesty, but for the moment there was the little matter of her gloves. These were as much of a challenge as the stockings had been, working fingers into the separate stalls one at a time and pulling the latex taut with deliberate care, fearful it might rip. Lianne understood now exactly what Ellen had meant when she had said that putting on such garments without the aid of talcum powder would have been well nigh impossible.

As with the stockings, the gloves were ultra long, reaching to the very limit of Lianne's arms. She flexed her fingers experimentally, wondering at the curious effect the rubber seemed to have on her appearance. She looked at herself in the mirror, then across to her handbag, wishing there was still something left in the vodka bottle to help combat the heart-thumping attack of nerves that was threatening to overwhelm her.

Ellen had only just taken the boots from the wardrobe when the door opened and a chubby-faced girl of about twenty entered. She had short cropped, mousy-coloured hair, and was probably about a stone too heavy to be wearing the figure hugging grey lycra leggings and the crop top which did nothing to restrain her ample breasts, but she had a cheery expression and a pleasantly musical voice when she spoke.

'Sorry I'm a bit behind with things,' she said, depositing

a large vanity case onto the bed. 'Sir wasn't very happy with the eye-shadow I used on Cindy; made me clean it all off and start from scratch. Fussy bastard.'

'This is Suzy, our makeup expert,' Ellen explained. 'And this is Lianne, our latest recruit,' she added, completing the introductions.

'Pleased to meet you,' Suzy said, extending a hand in greeting. Self consciously, because of the rubber gloves, Lianne extended her own hand in return. The contact felt strangely remote, though not unpleasant. She wondered what the cherubic makeup girl made of her, standing there feeling more exposed than when she had been naked, but concluded Suzy must have seen it all before, many times over.

'Nice hair,' Suzy commented, scrutinising Lianne professionally. 'How do you normally wear it?'

'Just as it is now,' Lianne replied, a note of surprise in her voice. Suzy pursed her lips and then made a clucking sound with her tongue.

'Bit of a waste, isn't it?' she commented. 'Never mind, let's have that ponytail down and see what Sister Suzy can do with it.'

Twenty minutes or so later, and Lianne had to admit she liked what "Sister Suzy" could do. She had backcombed, teased, and cajoled, until Lianne's normally tame, straight locks shone lustrously and looked silky soft.

'Bloody good, aren't I?' Suzy said smugly, seeing the clear look of approval on Lianne's face when she finally stood and turned to see herself in the mirror.

'Yes – it's quite amazing.'

'Right then, makeup,' Suzy announced and guided her back to sit on the side of the bed. She took a smaller case from inside the large one and opened it, laying it next to Lianne, and began to work her magic once more. First there were the false eyelashes, like a pair of mutant spiders. Lianne doubted whether any adhesive could possibly hold them for long, but when she suggested this to Suzy the girl simply laughed.

'We use nothing but the best of anything here,' she reassured her. 'These will stay where I put 'em till hell freezes over, or longer, without the solvent. Now hold still. If I get this wrong it'll take ages to clean them off again.'

Once the lashes had been anchored in place, Suzy applied thick black mascara, blending them in with the base of Lianne's eyelids and extending a small line wide of each one. She then began with the various eye-shadows, blending dark and light blues and touches of pink. Lianne wished she could see what she was actually doing to her, but Suzy had positioned her on the side of the bed nearer the door with her back to the mirror, so she had to remain patient until the job was completed.

That was done with the application of a lipstick that was the most vivid red Lianne had ever seen; far more lurid than she would ever have dared wear under normal circumstances. Not even content with that, Suzy then added a gloss sealer that Lianne knew would emphasise the colour even more. When she was finally allowed to see the overall effect she was so staggered she let out an involuntary squeal of disbelief.

'Bloody hell!' she breathed. 'What have you done?' She continued to stare at herself – her new self – unable to believe what Suzy had done. In place of the fairly ordinary, if basically pretty, girl that Lianne was used to seeing every morning, was now a pouting vixen with large fantastic eyes and a wide slash of a mouth. 'Bloody hell,' she repeated at last. 'Whatever do I look like?'

'Absolutely fantastic,' Ellen put in. 'The punters will love you.' Which was a lot more than Lianne could say of her own reaction to the boots when Ellen finally put them on her feet. The heels were like twin rapiers. They were at least five inches high and arched her feet to an almost impossible degree. They laced tightly into place, but there was also a broad ankle strap, in one end of which there was a slot that fitted over a steel staple in the other end. Then to Lianne's further astonishment Ellen slipped a small padlock through each and clicked them shut, preventing her from removing the footwear.

'Is that really necessary?' she demanded. Ellen nodded.

'We have to get the proper effect,' she said. 'In the scenes we're doing today we're both prisoners of the wicked lady and her gang, and they're forcing us to become their sex slaves.'

'That's ridiculous,' Lianne protested. 'I've never heard such nonsense. Who would pay out good money to see something like that?'

'You'd be surprised,' Suzy interjected. 'And it's not as ridiculous as you think. Men love women to dress up and a lot of women love doing it – me included. The only problem with me is I just don't have the figure for it. You don't know how lucky you are.' Standing in front of the mirror, perched on the precarious heels, Lianne was not sure she agreed with Suzy's definition of "lucky", though she was forced to admit that she did present an impressive picture.

Suzy now turned her attention to Ellen, but did not have to spend quite so long on her brunette hair, which

16

she simply coiled up and pinned atop her head and then lacquered for good measure. She did, however, do as thorough a job with her makeup. Again she used the long lashes and masses of mascara and shadow, creating a finished effect as dramatic as the one she had achieved with Lianne, though the eye-shadow created a dark red, glowing impression and the lipstick and gloss were jet black.

'Right then, I'll leave you girls to it for now,' Suzy said, closing up her case. 'Unless you want me to give you a bit of a trim down there,' she offered Ellen, indicating the dark thatch of hair between the tops of her thighs. Ellen shook her head.

'No, thanks all the same,' she replied. 'I'm supposed to be as I am for these shots.'

Suzy nodded. 'Oh, one of those scenes, is it?' she said mysteriously, though Ellen seemed to understand what she meant, for she nodded and grinned as the plump girl headed towards the bedroom door.

Ellen's costume was also made of rubber, but completely different from Lianne's in that it was a one piece catsuit that covered her from toes to head. The bodice was molded with cups that held her full breasts firmly, the thin fabric emphasising rather than concealing her proud nipples. The suit was an incredible piece of genius; the sleeves even terminating in gloves, and a zip through the crotch allowing access to Ellen's sex, if required. It was made to fit very tightly, and Lianne had to struggle to close the heavy zip at the back.

'At least it's not as tight as this damned corset,' Lianne grumbled whilst secretly admiring her friend's sleek outline. Ellen grinned.

'There's more to come,' she said, turning to the

wardrobe. She returned carrying a pair of long rubber boots and something that resembled a wide belt. She wrapped it around herself and fastened it across her stomach, buckling the two thinner straps that were provided for the purpose. When she turned around, Lianne saw that there were laces at the back to enable it to be tightened even further.

'Well don't just stand there, silly,' Ellen said. 'Get lacing, all the way closed. This'll bring my waist down to the same as yours is now, and I'm an inch bigger to start with, so you'll have to give it all you've got.' Lianne did just that, though at first she did not think she would be able to make it. Eventually, red in the face beneath her makeup, she was able to knot off the laces and take a breather. Ellen sat on the edge of the bed and began drawing the first boot up her left leg.

The boots were made of the same thick black rubber as Lianne's corset. Lacing each one took quite a while, and it was fully ten minutes before Ellen finally rose to parade back and forth. The heels were equally as high as those Lianne was wearing, and yet the older girl was able to walk without any difficulty at all.

'Practice,' Ellen replied, when Lianne commented on this. 'You'll get used to it yourself soon enough. Now, where did I leave those collars?'

The collars proved to be the final touch to both their costumes. Ellen's fitted over the neckline of her suit, and Lianne's buckled about her bare throat. They were both made from rubber. Lianne looked at her flatmate and then at her own reflection across the room, and shook her head in bewilderment.

'What the hell am I doing here, looking like this?' she breathed. Ellen placed a reassuring arm around her shoulder.

'Earning a living, you daft cow,' she said, 'same as I am. Now, you practice in those heels whilst I nip down the corridor for a pee. Thank heavens for detachable crotch flaps,' she added, laughing as she made for the door.

Lianne blew out another cloud of smoke and turned to look for an ashtray in which to stub out the cigarette. It really did taste awful and it wasn't doing anything to help her nerves anyway. She wondered if it were possible to get a drink – an alcoholic drink – before they moved on to whatever came next. When Ellen returned from the bathroom she ventured the question. Ellen winked and went to the second wardrobe, emerging from it with a large bottle and two plastic beakers.

'Not vodka I'm afraid,' she said, 'and not even a really good brandy, but it's better than nothing and Nadia does provide it for free.'

'Does she get a lot of models with bad nerves then?' Lianne asked, grabbing the first beaker from Ellen and gulping down the contents greedily. The liquid burned her throat even more than the vodka had done earlier, but it felt warm as it reached her stomach and she mentally crossed her fingers that it would do the trick. Ellen was sipping at her own beaker in a far more ladylike manner.

'Modelling can be a stressful game at the best of times,' she said. 'And this game is something different again. With these outfits you have to go for whole sequences in one shoot, or else keep them on between times. It takes so long to get in and out of this stuff it's better to get it over with in one. A drop of brandy not only steadies the nerves, it stiffens the resolve.' She walked over to the chest of drawers and consulted the wristwatch she had abandoned there earlier.

'If you get that down your neck,' she said, nodding to the beaker that Lianne was still clutching, 'you'll just about have time for a quickie refill. Only for God's sake don't go falling downstairs in those heels. You wouldn't be the first girl to do her ankles some serious damage.'

CHAPTER TWO

The studio "set" for the day's session was situated in one of the cavernous cellars that honeycombed the ground beneath the house. Ellen led the way, though this time their route avoided the main staircases, going down instead by way of a narrow spiral staircase, which seemed to Lianne, clinging to the handrail and taking each downward step with exaggerated care, to go on forever.

The cellar was a gothic nightmare, the walls painted black and the light coming from a series of red lamps set into the ceiling and walls. It did not look anywhere near bright enough for taking photographs, but Lianne noticed the two umbrella-style photographic floods that stood to either side, and reasoned that there would be plenty of light when they were switched on.

Apart from the photographer they were the first to arrive, and Ellen lost no time in making the introductions. Simon Prescott was probably only in his mid-thirties, but his reddish blond hair was already thinning and receding at the front at an alarming rate. He was very tall – taller even than Ellen in her steepling heels – and as thin as a rake; the flesh stretched taut over his cheekbones, his eyes pale and gaunt. He seemed friendly enough however, and exchanged handshakes with Lianne in a way she found preposterously formal, given the way she was dressed and presented. His lingering inspection of her betrayed his approval for what he saw, however.

'Very nice,' he said, understating to the power of ten. 'Very nice indeed. You'll make the ideal Marylou. Where did you say you found her, Ellen?'

'Lianne and I share a flat,' Ellen replied, 'and, just between ourselves, she's never done any of this stuff before, so go easy on her. I know how bitchy you can be at times.' It appeared to Lianne that Ellen and Simon knew each other more than passably well and she wondered just how many of these sessions her friend had done previously. Quite a few, she guessed, judging not only from the ease with which she handled the high heels, but also from the confident manner in which she paraded herself. Well, she thought, if Ellen can keep coming back for more, maybe it can't be all that bad.

She turned away, leaving the two of them in conversation, and peered into the gloom. The first thing she made out, however, gave her serious cause to reconsider that last judgement. Hesitantly, she took a couple of paces towards it, staring open-mouthed in horrified fascination.

Basically it was a chair; a heavy timber construction with a high back and sturdy, leather padded arms. The seat was high enough to prevent anyone using it from touching the floor with anything more than the tips of their toes, and there were thick straps on the front legs, the arms and the back, that were clearly intended to restrain the sitter. But it was not the straps that were causing Lianne's heart to pound against her ribs. It was the thick, unmistakably phallic shaft that rose nine or ten inches from the middle of the seat itself.

She took another few paces forward, her knees trembling, still not quite able to believe the evidence of her eyes. But there could be no doubting it. The only way anyone would be able to sit in that seat was if the thick black shaft was embedded deep inside their most intimate place.

'You can try it out if you like.' The voice close behind Lianne made her start and let out a little gasp. She turned to find Nadia Muirhead there, her arms folded across her chest, a curious smile dancing on her lips. She nodded towards the chair. 'I said, you can try it out if you like,' she repeated. Lianne took a couple of backward steps, shaking her head in disbelief.

'N – no,' she stammered. 'No thank you.'

Nadia shrugged. 'Ah well,' she said, 'each to her own, I suppose. Shame really, because it's a beautiful piece, don't you think? Completely hand made and impossible to escape from. Even an escapologist would be stumped on that.'

'I think an escapologist would have trouble sitting on it in the first place,' Lianne heard herself say.

Nadia chuckled. 'Oh, I don't know so much,' she said, enigmatically. She looked Lianne up and down. 'Anyway, I see you're ready for action, at least. Yes… very nice too. I see the others aren't here yet, so you may as well carry on looking around whilst we're waiting. Some of our little props are quite novel, but things will be explained when the time comes.' She moved away to talk to Simon, and Ellen detached herself and rejoined Lianne. Still somewhat shaken by Nadia's suggestion, Lianne grabbed hold of her friend's arm and pointed to the chair.

'Do you know what that woman just said to me?' she said incredulously. Ellen's face remained impassive as she replied.

'I'd imagine she asked if you wanted to try the chair,' she said. 'And I can imagine your reaction to that, too.'

'Well, it's not bloody surprising, is it? I mean, can you imagine trying to sit on that – that *thing*?'

Ellen's lips twitched, almost imperceptibly. 'Who needs to imagine?' she replied quietly. Lianne stared at her, aghast.

'You don't mean – you don't mean that – that you...?'

Ellen nodded. 'Twice.' Lianne barely managed to choke back a cry of abhorrence at her friend's calm revelation. She stared at her, shaking her head in fascinated disbelief. 'And,' Ellen went on after a brief pause to let her admission sink in, 'it was actually rather fun. The cock vibrates, you know. I had a terrific orgasm that went on for ages. Simon and James said it was one of the best pictures ever.'

Lianne was beginning to think she was going crazy. 'You mean – you mean you sat on that thing and – and, you know, with all those people watching? How could you?'

'Easy. Same as you, I had a couple of good stiffeners first and anyway, I was a bit turned on by the scenes we'd already shot that day.'

Lianne let out a derisory snort. 'Well, I'm not doing anything like that, and if anyone suggests it I'm out of here like a shot. I thought we were just supposed to be posing.' Ellen patted her arm.

'No one will ask you to do anything against your will,' she said. 'Though once you get a bit more used to all this you'll probably loosen up a bit. Don't think I just walked in on my first day and jumped straight in. All you'll be doing today is a bit of bondage.'

'Bondage?' Lianne echoed. 'You mean chains and stuff?'

'And stuff,' Ellen agreed. 'Nothing painful; just pretty lady struggling in her bonds, nasty villains standing about brandishing whips and the like. All you have to do is pretend to look terrified.'

'Who'll need to pretend?' Lianne retorted. 'I'm bloody terrified already.'

Their brief exchange was interrupted by the arrival of two more girls who, judging by their costumes, were obviously more cast members. They greeted Ellen cheerily and came across to introduce themselves to Lianne. The taller girl, Carla Wayne, was a deep ebony colour with long black lustrous hair. She was also the tallest woman Lianne had ever met, and even without the spike heels on her thigh-length boots, stood well over six feet tall. Her costume was sheer fetish fantasy. Apart from the long white boots, she wore a tight white corset, also made of leather, which was only just holding its own in the battle to support and constrain her massive breasts, and white kid gloves that reached to her shoulders. About her throat was a white collar from which a circle of vicious looking spikes protruded at least three inches. Her smile of welcome, however, belied her appearance, baring a set of the most even white teeth Lianne had seen.

'Hi,' she said. 'I'm the nasty bad lady who gets to tie

you up and whip you. Nothing personal, of course.' She laughed and jerked her head towards her companion. 'Meet my sidekick, Dolores – better known as Hazel O'Dee, one time cabaret singer and occasional stripper. I'm Carla by the way – Madame B in the script.'

Hazel was also very tall, though by comparison with Carla it would have been easy to think otherwise. She had thick, curly red hair which, to judge from her slightly freckled complexion, was the real thing and not out of a bottle. She was also wearing white leather, including long boots, but the rest of her outfit comprised a flared mini dress that reminded Lianne of the sort of thing woman ice skaters wore on television. It had long, close fitting sleeves, a plunging neckline that revealed most of her generous cleavage, and was so short that the tops of her boots were clearly visible every time she moved. Her appearance was so stunning that, when she spoke to reveal a broad Birmingham accent, Lianne was taken totally by surprise.

'Dolores is usually the gofer,' she explained. 'Show off a bit of body and try to look stern and stupid at the same time. I can manage the second bit easily enough, but I'm afraid I get fits of the giggles some times. Paul – he's the writer – keeps losing his temper with me and threatening to write some scenes where Carla makes me wear a gag for being too kind to the prisoners. Mind you, he's a right bastard and I reckon he believes all women should be gagged permanently.'

'Sometimes I think he might have a good point,' cut in a deep voice from the gloom in the direction of the doorway. Lianne looked around sharply and got her first glimpse of the leading man, all six feet three, well muscled, bleached-blond hair of him. From the waist down he was encased in tight leather polished trousers tucked into heavy-soled stormtrooper boots, but from the waist up he was naked, apart from a collar similar to Carla's. He had a face that could have been handsome, but for the broken nose and the slightly too thick bottom lip, but his torso could have graced the cover of any "bodice ripper" novel anywhere.

'Gavin,' he said, advancing towards Lianne. 'Gavin Cross. And you must be the new victim – Lianne, isn't it?'

The way his eyes devoured her rubber covered body made Lianne cringe, but she fought back the feeling and accepted the proffered handshake. At least, she thought, everyone was politely professional, so maybe it wasn't so bad, though the formality with which the various introductions had been made was more than a little incongruous, given the setting and situation.

The party was completed a few moments later by the arrival of two more men who, Lianne quickly learned, were the writer Paul Dean and the artist who produced the finished illustrations, James Naylor. Paul was tall and dark-haired, and his face wore the sort of expression that suggested he might at any time break into a fit of laughter. He was neither thin nor heavily built; just a sort of average man in the street. But there was something about the way his eyes danced and sparkled with apparently suppressed amusement that Lianne found compulsive. James on the other hand had sharp features emphasised by a hawkish nose, had a paunch that was out of place on his otherwise fairly lightweight frame, and had greying hair. Lianne guessed that he was also a heavy drinker, for his cheeks bore the florid look of a man who spends too much time looking down a bottle.

Seeing that everyone was assembled, Nadia clapped her hands for attention and they all gathered round. She surveyed the gathering twice, like a schoolmistress making sure that none of her charges had strayed before the homeward coach was boarded, and nodded approvingly.

'Right then, boys and girls,' she said, 'you've all met Lianne, our new Marylou, so let's get down to it. Poor Stacey's unfortunate illness has thrown us a day behind schedule, so we'll all have to work that little bit harder to make up for it. Now, Paul has slightly revised his script, so let's get to it.'

They dispersed in various directions and Lianne just had a glimpse of Gavin and James disappearing behind a heavy curtain that screened the end wall before she found herself face to face with the redheaded Hazel. To Lianne's horror she was holding up some sort of leather harness, which she plainly intended to put on her. The taller girl obviously registered the panic in Lianne's eyes, for she lowered her burden a little and leaned closer, whispering conspiratorially.

'I guess this stuff is new to you, yeah?' she said. 'Well look, don't get scared. It's just a load of straps, but no one will hurt you, not really. Just turn around and I'll fasten you up, only if madame thinks we're wasting time she's likely to throw a right wobbler.'

Taking as deep a breath as her corset would allow, Lianne slowly turned her back on Hazel, closing her eyes and wishing she were anywhere but where she was. The effect of the drinks seemed to have worn off far to quickly, banished by the sight of the awful chair and now this. She swallowed hard as Hazel adjusted the heavy collar about her throat, buckling it over the rubber one she already wore, shifting slightly as she felt the leather strap rubbing against the bare skin between her shoulder-blades. As Hazel gently guided her right wrist into the first leather manacle, Lianne opened her eyes again and saw that a few feet away Carla was immobilising Ellen's upper limbs, although in her case the heavy collar held two smaller straps which were being used to bind Ellen's wrists to either side of her neck. Her flatmate did not seem at all perturbed over the routine and was smiling and talking quietly to her fictional captor.

Behind Lianne's back, Hazel had quickly secured her other wrist and was now buckling another strap about her upper arm, just above the elbow, pulling the joint back uncomfortably. When the second elbow was pinioned in the same way and the lateral strap which joined them cinched tighter, Lianne's shoulders were pulled back so far that she was forced to stand in a position which thrust her breasts out in a fashion she thought most vulgar.

'Comfortable?' Hazel asked, moving around in front of her.

'Hardly,' Lianne muttered. 'You want to try being in my position and you'd know.'

Hazel arched her eyebrows. 'Oh, I have,' she said. 'Only I haven't got quite such prominent tits as you, unfortunately. I must say, the part definitely suits you. You look good enough to eat.'

'Can't you loosen this off a bit?' Lianne pleaded. Hazel shook her head.

'Simon and James would have my guts for garters if I did,' she said. 'They reckon if it doesn't look real then it's no good. Simon has to get the photograph just right, or else James can't produce a realistic finished article. Sorry, but that's what they pay us for. We have to suffer for our money, as well as for our art.'

Just across the room Carla had now manacled Ellen's ankles, hobbling her with a short length of chain and, to Lianne's total disbelief, was in the process of pushing a rubber ball between her teeth and buckling a strap about her head to keep it there. As she tightened the buckle, forcing the ball deeper still, Ellen's face took on a look of horrified surprise, though the wink she gave Lianne when she saw her watching suggested she was calmly in control of the situation.

Lianne was just beginning to wonder what it must feel like to be gagged in such a cruel way when she found out first hand. Hazel had moved behind her again and she struck so fast that Lianne had no chance to even try to resist. Strong fingers prised her mouth open, hard rubber was pushed home, and the strap was buckled tightly. With eyes even wider than Ellen's, Lianne looked from side to side, grunting in protest. Behind her, Hazel chuckled.

'Save that for the cameras,' she said, and Lianne realised that she genuinely did not understand that she was frightened out of her wits. The trouble was, now there was no way she could communicate that fact. For the time being, at least, she really was a helpless captive. The sudden realisation of that fact, however, had a totally unexpected effect on her. Despite the fact that her knees were trembling more violently than ever, a sudden wave of warmth swept upwards from her loins and, to her chagrin, she knew she was becoming hot and wet between her legs.

She became even more conscious of her position when Paul Dean sauntered over to her, remembering the comment earlier that he probably thought all women should be permanently gagged. There was a trace of a smile on his lips as he stopped in front of her, waving a sheaf of papers under her nose.

'Right then, Marylou,' he said, 'I can see you take to the gag very nicely. I just love that surprised look a ball gag brings to the eyes of the wearer, and those lovely big eyes of yours are perfect for the part. Now, your role is fairly simple, you just do as you're told and go where you're put. You can struggle and scream all you want; the sound part may be irrelevant, but it helps get the right feel for the photographs, and hence James' artwork afterwards. Oh, and I like these,' he said, suddenly tweaking Lianne's left breast. The rubber bra cup was enough to prevent any real sensation of touch, but the cavalier attitude would have left Lianne speechless even had she not already been deprived of the power of that faculty.

Hazel grasped Lianne's arm and turned her back towards the actual set area where Simon had now set up two separate cameras, in addition to the one he wore slung around his neck. While Hazel had been busy rendering her helpless, Gavin and James had dragged a heavy wooden framework from behind the curtain and set it up in the centre of the two umbrella lights. It was a fairly basic structure; two sturdy A-frames supporting a four foot cross member a little more than six feet from the floor. But, as Lianne watched goggle-eyed, Gavin brought a stepladder, climbed two steps up and began fastening a pulley block a few inches from one end of the horizontal beam, using a short length of chain and a long steel bolt which James passed up to him.

He tugged on the mounting, making sure it held fast, and then climbed down and moved the stepladder until it stood directly under the opposite end of the frame, whereupon he quickly repeated the process with a second pulley. As he dismounted his perch for the second time the two floodlights suddenly blazed into life, bathing the whole scene in a harsh white radiance and throwing stark shadows against the walls as the various players moved about. To her left, Lianne was aware of Ellen being pushed up alongside her and turned her head towards her friend, trying to signal to her with her eyes. If Ellen understood the sheer panic that was threatening to engulf her she gave no indication of it, simply winking and then turning back to watch the preparations "on stage".

By this time Gavin had passed two stout ropes over the grooved wheels of the respective pulleys, drawing the loose ends down until they trailed on the stone floor and tying the other ends off to the nearer A-frame. He then moved away to a low bench against one wall and rummaged amongst the pile of things that had been apparently thrown there earlier. He had his back to the room as he dipped his head and Lianne's view was obstructed as he lifted something up and began pulling it over his close-cropped skull. She saw something black and the glint of something metallic, and only guessed what it was a split second before he turned again to reveal that his entire face and head was now obscured by a black leather hood, through which only his eyes and mouth were visible. The effect was so sinister that Lianne very nearly lost control of her bladder and the shaking in her legs began to get worse again.

To Lianne's consternation he made straight for her, looming up in front of her and placing his large hands on her naked shoulders. She flinched at his touch, but her obvious fear only served to make him snigger aloud.

'Aha,' he said, in a deep stage voice, 'so the little witch cannot abide the flesh of her Nemesis. Very well, so be it.' He wheeled away and went back to the bench, and this time when he returned Lianne saw he had pulled on a pair of heavy, studded gauntlets. Her stomach went cold at the sight of them and she thought she was going to faint when he took her shoulders into their tight leather grip.

'Methinks the wench protests too much,' Gavin intoned melodramatically. Lianne whimpered through her gag and closed her eyes tightly, but suddenly he was laughing and patting her shoulders gently.

'You're a damned good actress,' he said, 'I'll give you that much. This is going to be a rare pleasure.'

Lianne opened her eyes again and stared up at him. The mask hid most of his features, but there was no mistaking the fact that he was smiling and his eyes glinted mischievously. Good god, she thought to herself, he really does think I'm putting this on! He really doesn't understand that I'm scared half to death by all this and I can't bloody well tell him otherwise!

Simon's cameras were already clicking as Hazel and Gavin led Lianne forward, positioning her beneath the frame and turning her to face the small group of expectant faces that were fixed exclusively on her. Carla stepped forward carrying a long metal tube, from each end of which dangled a thick leather strap. She paused, looking Lianne up and down.

'Better get her panties off now,' she said to Hazel.

'Once this is on it'll be impossible.' Lianne gave a strangled cry on hearing this and tried to pull away, but Gavin held her firmly and there was little chance of breaking his hold. She considered trying to kick out at Hazel, but the idea of violence had always been abhorrent to her and she hesitated to hurt another human being, no matter what the reason. The hesitation was all Hazel needed. She stooped, swept Lianne's legs up under her arm in one easy movement and, with her free hand, deftly began easing the thin latex briefs down her thighs. Suspended between the two of them, Lianne did not dare struggle, for fear of making Gavin lose his grip and sending her crashing onto the hard floor below. All she could do was hang limply while the tall redhead bared her most intimate parts to the audience and the waiting cameras.

When Hazel lowered her feet again, Lianne tried to press her thighs as tightly together as possible to minimise the invasion of her privacy. But even that comfort was quickly denied her. Passing the unwanted rubber panties to Carla, Hazel took the long bar from her in exchange and, kneeling down, rapidly fastened one end to Lianne's right ankle, using the heavy strap and pulling it as tightly as it would go. Looking down, Lianne saw that the leather was lined with some sort of dark fur, but she could not feel it through the latex stocking.

It was fortunate that Gavin maintained his grip on her, for when Hazel grabbed her other ankle and began dragging it away from the first she would certainly have fallen, so far apart did the redhead force her legs. Before Lianne had a chance to recover and try to return the leg to its original position, the second strap was buckled and there was no way she could close her legs again.

She let out a little groan of mortification, for now her sex was in full view and completely vulnerable. She saw Paul the writer, his eyes fixed intently upon her, and her cheeks flushed an even deeper red for his eyes held no amusement now, only desire and lust. Lianne shivered, realising that any one of them could take her as she was now and she would be powerless to resist. A sudden convulsion in the pit of her stomach sent another wave surging through her body, but this time it was something completely different.

As she returned Paul's stare she could not believe the thoughts that were cascading through her confused brain. To her utter amazement she realised that she wanted him to take her. She actually wanted him to step forward, remove his clothes, and plunge his cock into her defenceless body and ravish her in front of the whole crowd! She shook her head, fighting the notion for all she was worth, and she was so fully occupied with trying to deny the effect that all this was having on her that she did not notice the two ropes being tied to either end of the metal spreader bar. Only when Hazel and Carla began hauling on them, lifting her booted feet from the floor and forcing her to fall back into Gavin's arms, did she realise their intention.

She screamed, trying to make them stop, but her cries merely brought a ragged round of applause from those people not actively engaged in the tableau and one cry of 'Bravo!' from the artist, James. Lianne began to whimper in terror as the bar continued to rise, not believing this was really happening to her, even when the two girls secured the ropes, leaving her dangling upside down, her soft hair swaying a good foot above the floor, her back now to the audience.

'Nice butt,' she dimly heard someone say. 'Turn the whole thing around and let's see her face.' As the initial terror gave way to simple fear, Lianne realised that the speaker was Paul and, looking down, she saw that the base of the frame was set on small castors, making it very easy for Gavin and Hazel to comply with his instruction. As the frame was rotated and the others came into her upside down field of vision, Lianne saw the unmistakable expression of triumph on Paul's face, but she still wished it was he and not Gavin who began slowly stroking her sex lips with his leather-sheathed fingers.

This couldn't really be happening, her brain screamed, but when she looked back up her body she saw that gravity had dragged her breasts from their rubber cups and her nipples were now as exposed as her poor sex. Strangely, the sight of the erect pink tips pointing towards her face sent little tingles of excitement running through her and, as Gavin's index finger probed her labial lips gently apart, she realised that this whole performance was really beginning to excite her. When he knelt down before her, unzipped his trousers to reveal an impressive erection, and quickly removed her gag, she made no protest. As he guided the purplish knob towards her mouth she instinctively opened her lips and sucked him greedily inside.

From another world a voice was calling out instructions. She thought it sounded like Paul, though she no longer cared. A second voice, female – probably Nadia, perhaps Carla – joined in.

'Steady with her – not too fast!' It was definitely Nadia.

'Close up on this please, Simon,' directed Paul Dean.

'Pull her nipples. No, not like that, really pull them. Yes, that's better.' The initial pain of Gavin's gloved fingers mauling her sensitive flesh quickly gave way to a different sensation. She sucked greedily on his cock, bringing a fresh wave of orders ringing through the cellar.

'Easy there. Don't lose it yet.'

'Close up from above, Simon. Yeah, that's it.'

'Excellent. Keep holding it, Gavin. I'll say when.'

'Get Ellen's gag changed, this is giving me an idea!' That was definitely Paul, but Lianne was paying no attention now to anything other than her breasts, the urgent signals her empty cunt was sending to her brain, and the swollen shaft which filled her mouth. With an effort she managed to pull her head back, freeing her mouth momentarily from obstruction.

'Please!' she heard a beseeching voice wail. 'Please, for god's sake fuck me!' As Gavin guided his member back between her lips once again, Lianne realised the voice had been hers, though she had no recollection of the intent. *Slut! Dirty little slut, hung up like a piece of meat and bloody well enjoying it! Yes, yes, enjoying it! And why not? I can't do anything about it, can I? Yes, bloody well enjoy it, only will someone please fuck me, before I go stark raving mad!*

Suddenly Gavin withdrew with a gasp of relief. Lianne looked up at him, her eyes imploring him to satisfy her craving, not daring to trust her voice. He stood slightly to one side of her and she tensed, expecting them to lower her so that he could finish what he had started, but instead, she saw Ellen standing there – Ellen, with a huge black cock sticking out from where her mouth should have been. With a start Lianne saw that it was some sort of gag, held in place by a strap similar to the

36

ones which had held their original ball gags.

Carla was urging her forward, pushing her closer to Lianne who, suddenly realising what was intended, found her voice again.

'No,' she squealed. 'Don't make her do that. You can't!'

But they could – and they did, though there was evidently not much persuasion needed on Ellen's part, for she stepped up quickly, lowered her head, and began probing the lips of Lianne's sex with the tip of the rubber dildo.

'Help her, Carla, you great trollop,' someone called out and into Lianne's inverted field of vision came a white gloved hand, the fingers curling about the black shaft and guiding it towards its target. For a brief second Lianne tensed her muscles, intending to fight against this intrusion, but another finger suddenly pressed itself hard against the puckered ring of her bottom-hole and this distraction proved her undoing. The end of the rubber cock forced an entrance, Ellen thrust downwards and the entire monster slid into Lianne's slippery tunnel without further resistance.

A moment later Gavin was back on his knees before her, pushing Ellen's legs into a straddled stance to allow him to present his own cock again.

'Bastard!' Lianne hissed, but she vacuumed him into her mouth again, all the same. Now, with Ellen pumping the dildo and Gavin thrusting in and out of her mouth, his fingers back on her nipples, Lianne was rapidly losing control – but she no longer cared. Neither did she care when Gavin came, pumping a stream of salty semen into her throat. She swallowed, but her mouth refused to release its grip on him until she had finally finished the mind blowing orgasm which hit her like a runaway truck and blocked everything else in the world out of existence for long minutes.

Lianne was not sure whether she actually lost consciousness or whether she was just so overwhelmed by the violence of her climax, but she had no recollection of being lowered from the bar and her ankles being unstrapped. Someone was supporting her from behind and she was slumped against another body in front of her, but she had no idea who was who, or who it was who hoisted her between them. She was only dimly aware that someone had replaced her gag and it was only at the last minute, when she saw the chair had been dragged into the illuminated area, that she realised what they intended.

As they turned her about and positioned her over the seat and the waiting dildo, she tried to cry out for them to stop and made a feeble attempt at resistance, but the bonds on her arms and wrists rendered her completely helpless. She turned her head wildly from side to side, finally identifying her two captors as Gavin and Carla. Each had a hand under her lower thigh and another gripping her upper arm so that she was being supported in the sitting position and, as they began to lower her, Hazel stepped between her splayed thighs and stooped to guide her onto the long, thick shaft.

Her vagina was still so wet it was pointless even trying to clench her muscles against the intruder. The tip slid in without hindrance. As they lowered her further she let out a groan that was part protest, part desire, for the black cock was bigger than anything she had ever known before. By the time her buttocks settled on the seat itself she was astonished that the monstrous thing had not split her in two.

Busy hands buckled a wide strap across the top of her thighs, whilst others secured her ankles and still more were behind her, loosening the original harness and guiding her wrists into the leather cuffs on each of the chair's arms. The three of them worked so efficiently and expertly that the entire process took no more than seconds before they withdrew, leaving Lianne securely pinioned and plugged, unable to lift herself clear of the rubber cock.

'Make sure you get some good shots of that expression,' she heard Nadia call to Simon. 'That's just perfect. No, not yet Gavin!'

For several interminable seconds Lianne just sat, glaring towards the lights, the various figures silhouetted starkly against the glare and all but anonymous as they moved about. There were several flashes as Simon went about his work and hands from behind her reached around to lift her breasts clear of the rubber cups once more. Lianne looked down, horrified as she saw the little crocodile clip, already open, homing in on her right nipple. She squealed even before the serrated jaws closed on the tender flesh, and squealed even louder when they did. Moments later her left nipple was similarly clipped. Waves of pain flooded through her, only to be replaced by a different sensation as the huge cock began to slowly vibrate.

CHAPTER THREE

Lianne woke up to find she was still strapped in the chair and still impaled on the rubber cock, although someone had removed the gag. The photographic floods had been turned off and only the dim red lamps once more lighted the cellar. It was also deserted.

Lianne turned her head from side to side, craning her neck in an attempt to look behind her, but there was no doubting the fact that she was alone. She flexed her arms experimentally against the straps, but the leather was as unyielding as ever and there was no way she was going to break free unless someone came back for her. She tried to ease her position, but the embedded dildo handicapped her attempt and she abandoned it, fighting back an urge to scream out for someone to come to help.

How long she had been asleep she had no way of telling. It might have been only a few minutes, it might have been hours, but she was astonished she had dropped off at all. Her last recollection was of the vibrator finally stopping as she was in the midst of what had to be her fourth orgasm in succession, and of her finally slumping in an exhausted heap, supported only by the strap that someone had buckled around her chest during the ordeal. The strap, like the gag, was gone now, but it scarcely increased the amount of movement available to her. She wondered what could have possessed them to leave her in this predicament and whether or not it was intended as some kind of test. If so, she decided, it was a damned cruel one, for she had already done everything they had asked of her, most of which she would never have considered. She still couldn't believe the way she had reacted earlier and, if it hadn't been for the irrefutable evidence of her costume, the bondage, and the monstrous rubber cock that was still stretching her love tunnel, she would have dismissed it as being just a nightmarish dream.

But had it been such a nightmare? There was no escaping the fact that she had actually enjoyed it, had taken animal pleasure from what they had done to her, letting loose some part of her psyche she had never dreamed existed. She stared down at her nipples and at the red marks where the clips had been. She remembered the delicious pleasure/pain when they had been put on and the way the inner monster had risen to claim its rights when the vibrator had started up – and a part of her wished it would start up again.

She shook her head, trying to push such thoughts from her mind, and considered what she should do next. Not that there were many options, she realised. She could either scream the place down, or simply sit patiently on her ravishment throne and wait. Were they watching her, secretly, waiting to see her reaction? Lianne peered around in the gloom, trying to see if there were any cameras, but decided that even if there were, the light would have been too bad for them to pick up any decent sort of image. She sighed deeply, the corset now feeling like a giant hand that was trying to squeeze the life out of her. Why didn't someone come?

She decided to compromise and turned her head in the direction of the door.

'Hello?' she called, tentatively. 'Hello? Is someone there?' She paused, listening intently. Nothing. 'Hello? Look, I'm bloody stiff and I've still got this damned thing stuck up me. I can take a joke, but this is going beyond funny. Hello?'

To her relief she heard footsteps beyond the door; the unmistakable sound of stiletto heels on stone. But the figure that entered gave her little cause for that initial relief. Lianne guessed it had to be Suzy, the makeup girl, for she was short and stocky, though the tight corset she wore over the rubber catsuit had done wonders for her waistline, and the heels on her knee length boots had added a good four inches to her height. Until she spoke, however, Lianne could not be positive, for her head was entirely covered by a rubber mask similar to the leather one Gavin had worn earlier, so that only her eyes and lips were visible. She stood in the doorway for several seconds before advancing further into the room to stand in front of Lianne.

'Well, Miss Hot Pants, so I hear,' she sneered. Lianne let out a long sigh, realising she had been anxiously holding her breath.

'Never mind about all that,' she said. 'Just undo these straps and let me up from here – please.' Suzy took a step forward, the red light gleaming dully on the polished rubber where it stretched over her ample figure.

'What's the matter?' she asked. 'Getting fed up with Jumbo already?'

'Jumbo?' For a second or two Lianne was confused, but the penny quickly dropped. 'If you mean this thing I'm perched on, well yes. Wouldn't you be?'

'Not after only an hour, no,' Suzy said. 'I've sat on Jumbo for three or four hours at a time.'

'You?' Lianne's eyebrows shot up. 'But I thought—'

'You thought I was just the dumpy little plain thing who did the makeup for all the pretty models,' Suzy cut in. 'Too fat and too ugly to put in front of the cameras, is that it?'

'No, I—'

'Oh, spare me the crap. I know what I am and yes, I'm hardly the model type, but I still have my own likes and dislikes. I happen to like dressing up in rubber and I don't look that fat in a corset.' She turned around, showing herself off. 'Some men like a big arse – a nice rubber-covered big arse especially, and when I put on this mask I could be anybody, now couldn't I?'

'Yes, I suppose you could,' Lianne agreed, hardly able to believe she was having this conversation. 'Now, will you please get me out of this?'

'In a minute,' Suzy said, making no move towards her. 'I just want to enjoy looking at you a bit longer and then, I think, I might just kiss you.'

'You might what?' Lianne exclaimed. 'What are you talking about?'

'I'd have thought you could understand plain English,' Suzy calmly replied. 'I said, I want to kiss you. Does that surprise you?'

'Well, yes.'

'Because you've never been propositioned by a lesbian before? Tell me, what would you do if you weren't so nicely packaged up? Run for it? Slap my face? Scratch my eyes out? Well, you can't can you?' Now she did move closer, coming to stand alongside the chair to Lianne's right. She extended a rubber-covered hand and began stroking the exposed nipple nearest to her. Lianne tried to shrink away, but she was totally trapped, unable to repel or avoid the girl's attentions.

'Oh look,' Suzy crooned, rolling the pink bud between thumb and forefinger, 'it's starting to go hard already. It must like me, don't you think?' Lianne groaned, screwing her eyes shut, not wanting to see the evidence of her body's betrayal.

'Don't...' she protested. 'Please don't. If you must kiss me, then kiss me and get it over with. Don't just paw me.' Suzy suddenly released the nipple and lashed out, slapping Lianne across the left cheek. It was not a hard blow, but the unexpectedness of it made Lianne's eyes water.

'There's no need to be nasty!' Suzy snapped, and the hard edge that had crept into her tone shocked Lianne. The rubber fingers sought the nipple again and resumed their attentions. Suzy's face loomed before Lianne's bewildered eyes, the heavily rouged lips moving against the black latex like some strange, independent creature. 'I'll kiss you when I'm good and ready and not before,' they said. 'And I think you should ask me to kiss you first – ask really politely.' She paused, waiting to see Lianne's reaction. The mouth moved closer still. 'Ask me, you arrogant bitch, or I'll switch Jumbo on again and have my tongue down your dirty little throat when you come.'

Lianne's eyes opened wide in horror. 'You wouldn't!' she gasped.

The red lips curled into a cruel smile.

'Try me. And you'd probably have your tongue down mine, from what I've heard about the way you reacted earlier. Or perhaps I should kneel up and let you tongue me instead?'

'No...' The plea came out as a strangled squeak, the

thought of what Suzy was threatening too dreadful to contemplate. Lianne struggled to control her voice. 'No,' she repeated in something nearer a normal voice. 'No, please... please, kiss me Suzy.'

'Say it again. Say "Please kiss me Suzy, and please put your tongue in my mouth".'

'Please kiss me Suzy... and please put your tongue in my—!'

Lianne never finished the sentence. Her mouth was suddenly covered by Suzy's, the girl's earnest tongue probing between her lips and seeking her own. At the same time the rubber fingers slipped from the nipple they had been pinching and delved between Lianne's thighs, searching urgently until the index finger found her clitoris and crushed it against the hard rubber cock. Lianne groaned and suddenly realised she was returning the kiss with rapidly increasing ardour, the now familiar tide once more rising to engulf her as Suzy began to expertly frig her.

CHAPTER FOUR

The rest of the cast and crew were sitting around in a large lounge overlooking the lawns when Suzy led Lianne back upstairs. She had managed to recover the latex panties that had been part of her original costume, but despite ransacking the cellar she had been unable to find anything else with which to attempt some sort of modesty. Worse still, the collar from the bondage harness was still locked about her neck, the rest of the straps dangling down her back. Suzy had denied any knowledge as to the whereabouts of the keys.

As the two of them entered the room Lianne saw that they were all dressed as before; everyone still in costume, including another girl Lianne had not met before. Gavin had removed his executioner's mask, but that was the only change. The new girl was wearing a brief little halter dress made from polished red leather, with red stockings and red boots to match. Her fingernails had been painted an identical colour, but her red hair was almost certainly its original colour. Deeper than Hazel's, it fell completely straight on either side of her face like an auburn curtain, or a sun burnished waterfall.

Several heads turned as Suzy ushered Lianne into the room, but it was Nadia who spoke first.

'Feeling a little better, my dear?' she asked, eyes twinkling. Lianne felt herself blushing, but decided attack was the best form of defence.

'I think you are a crowd of evil, sadistic, cruel—'

'Spare us, please,' Nadia said, raising a hand as if to ward off Lianne's words. 'We've heard it all before, believe me.'

'Well, what do you expect?' Lianne demanded. 'I came here to model for some sort of magazine project, and find myself done up like – like this,' she indicated her costume, 'and then find myself trussed up, hung up and – and—'

'And having more orgasms in one hour than you've probably had in the last month,' Nadia finished for her. 'Maybe even the last six months. Well, yes, I can imagine it's all come as a bit of a shock to you, but I really thought Ellen there had explained things better. So, I apologise for anything you found unacceptable and I will quite understand if you decide to leave.' Her hand disappeared into the depths of the armchair in which she was sitting and re-emerged holding a manila envelope, which she held out towards Lianne.

'What's that?' Lianne asked, her eyes narrowing suspiciously. Nadia smiled.

'It's your fee – not only for today, but for the rest of the week. You will find fourteen hundred pounds in fifty pound notes in here and it's yours, whether you choose to go now, or otherwise.'

With fingers trembling, Lianne stepped forward and took the proffered package. The latex gloves hampered her yet again as she fumbled to tear open the flap and she made an untidy mess of the paper as she finally ripped it open. As if in a dream she drew the contents half out, exposing the unmistakable pinkish red notes. For a few seconds she stood transfixed at the sight of them, and then quickly thrust them back out of sight.

'They're all real, too,' Paul Dean said languidly, hooking one leg casually over the arm of his chair. Beyond him Carla smiled encouragingly, her teeth a brilliant white against her dark face.

'The money's one of the few things that is real around here,' she laughed.

'You'll pay me for the rest of the week, even if I leave now?' Lianne asked incredulously. Nadia nodded.

'I believe I just did that very thing,' she replied quietly. 'Now, if you would prefer, you can have until morning to decide. You must be tired as well as hungry.' She indicated a long low sideboard against the far wall, upon which were set a number of glass covered trays piled high with sandwiches and rolls. 'You'll find plenty to eat over there, and there's either wine or coffee.' Lianne's gaze took in the percolator and the wine cooler. She turned back to look at Nadia again, her brain wrestling with a dozen conflicting emotions.

'Listen,' she said, trying to keep her voice level, 'I must be going slightly crazy here, but I accept your apology – sort of. The only thing is, if I do stay, I don't mind the dressing up bit and I suppose the bondage stuff is okay, though I wasn't too keen on being hung upside down like that. But what about all the other stuff?'

'The other stuff?' Nadia asked innocently.

Lianne nibbled her bottom lip, hesitating, trying to find the words. Her gaze travelled furtively around the room, but not one face betrayed a flicker of emotion.

'You know what I'm talking about,' she said at last. 'You *all* know what I'm talking about. What you did to me, and that obscene chair – that Jumbo *thing*. And her—' she added, jerking an accusatory thumb in the direction of Suzy, who had remained motionless by the door throughout the entire exchange.

'You mustn't mind Suzy,' Nadia said. 'She just prefers women to men, and she simply can't resist a lovely helpless one. I have told her about it before, but she never seems to listen. She'll be punished for that later, of course. You can watch if you like. You can even cane that fat little rump of hers yourself.'

Lianne shrank back, horrified. 'Cane her?' she echoed.

'Of course. Mind you, I think she actually enjoys it, don't you, you little strumpet?'

Lianne automatically turned towards Suzy, but the anonymous black figure made no reaction to Nadia's challenge. 'Anyway,' Nadia continued, 'forget about Suzy. As for what you call the "other stuff", I can't make any promises. We strive for realism here and I'm afraid certain things can't be faked. Besides, did you really find it all so horrible? It didn't look that way from where I was watching, I must say.'

CHAPTER FIVE

'I can't believe I actually agreed to stay here!' Lianne exclaimed. 'And I certainly didn't figure on sleeping over.'

'What's the problem with that?' Ellen asked, turning back the covers on the bed. 'Everything's switched off back at the flat, and we don't have newspapers or milk delivered. Think of the extra gas and electricity we're saving on.'

They were back upstairs in the bedroom where they had first changed earlier that day. The first thing Lianne did was snatch up the little bunch of keys that had been left on the chest of drawers and start searching for the ones which would release her from the collar and the torment of the boots.

Now, sitting on the end of the bed, the boots thrown against the wardrobe, she stretched her toes, still sheathed in the rubber stockings, relishing the freedom of movement and the terrific relief of not having her feet so painfully arched all the time. She decided she had earned a cigarette, and also had serious intentions towards whatever remained of the brandy tucked away in the second wardrobe. She looked about her, spotting her handbag on the stool by the window, but seeing no sign of the clothes in which she had arrived. Ellen's clothes were gone too, and when Lianne looked inside the wardrobes she found the only items there were made from either rubber or leather. She turned to Ellen who, apart from removing her own boots, had made no attempt to remove her costume.

'What's happened to my things?' she demanded. 'And yours? Someone's taken them all.'

Ellen smiled. 'Don't panic. One of the maids will have sent them all off to be laundered. They'll be back tomorrow afternoon.'

'Tomorrow afternoon? What if I had decided to leave this evening? What was I supposed to wear? I could hardly walk out dressed like this?'

'There are plenty of skirts and dresses in there,' Ellen replied. 'Take your pick.'

'But they're all rubber and stuff,' Lianne protested. 'And all the skirts I've seen are hardly what you'd call decent!'

'Decent is as decent does,' Ellen retorted, tossing her head back. 'Just put on a pair of latex tights underneath and your modesty will be intact enough.'

'I wouldn't dare go outside wearing rubber,' Lianne snorted. 'Everybody would think I was some kind of perve!'

'Which you're not, of course.'

Lianne wished fervently that she did not blush so easily and turned away to hide her embarrassment from her friend. 'There's no need to be sarcastic,' she retorted defensively. 'Besides, I wasn't exactly given much choice in proceedings, was I?'

'No, I know,' Ellen said. She moved across and laid a comforting hand on Lianne's arm. 'But you're still embarrassed, and not just about what happened, aren't you?'

'What do you think?' Lianne lowered her eyes, avoiding Ellen's direct gaze.

'I think,' Ellen replied softly, 'that you're more embarrassed that you kept coming like a tigress in heat and that everybody was watching you.'

'You could have stopped them,' Lianne protested.

'Me? In case you hadn't noticed, I was trussed up and gagged throughout the whole thing.'

'But you knew what to expect before that,' Lianne pointed out. 'You didn't even try to warn me.'

'And if I had?'

The room fell silent for several seconds. Ellen stroked Lianne's bare shoulder. 'You wouldn't have fourteen hundred smackers tucked in your knickers at this moment, for a start.'

'That makes me sound like some cheap sort of whore.'

'Hardly cheap and not a whore. You're an actress, like me.'

'That's the problem,' Lianne wailed. 'I wasn't acting, was I? Maybe everyone thought I was at the start, but they all found out the truth soon enough, and you all knew I was terrified of that chair.'

'Good old Jumbo,' Ellen whispered, half to herself.

'Bloody Jumbo!' Lianne snapped. 'The thing nearly split me in two. I can hardly walk with my legs together.'

'But you liked the end result?'

'"Liked" is not the word I would have chosen,' Lianne said. 'I lost control, the way anybody would with that thing buzzing away inside them. They took advantage of me when I couldn't resist.'

'That's the bit I like best,' Ellen replied. 'I can just let myself go and tell myself I can't be blamed, because I'm totally helpless. Isn't that what happened to you?'

There was a long pause, the two girls like erotic statues, Ellen's hand motionless on Lianne's shoulder. Slowly Lianne turned to face her flatmate, their faces only inches apart, their eyes locking.

'Yes,' she said, very quietly. 'That's exactly what happened. And this, too.' She reached out, embraced the taller girl, and kissed her on the lips, her tongue parting them and darting over her teeth in search of its opposite number. She felt Ellen's arms encircling her in return, drawing her close, her rubber hands pressing into the soft, exposed flesh of her buttocks, one finger exploring against the puckered ring of her bottom through the flimsy latex of her knickers.

Oh good grief! Lianne thought. Here we go again!

CHAPTER SIX

'Where are we going?' Lianne whispered into the darkness. Ahead of her, visible as little more than a darker shadow, Ellen stopped and raised a cautionary finger to her lips.

'Not so loud,' she admonished. 'All the actual cellars are soundproofed, but not these corridors and stairs. Noise carries for miles with all this smooth stone about.'

'But where are we actually going?' They had just descended a long circular stairwell, similar to the one by which they had gained access to the underground level that afternoon, and were standing in an unlit passageway that disappeared into the gloom. Lianne, heart thumping, peered in both directions, but could see nothing beyond the dark outline of her friend. Still wearing her black rubber catsuit, Ellen would have been invisible at anything more than a few feet, with only the pale skin of her face to possibly betray her presence. She reached out and grasped Lianne's arm.

'I told you, it's a surprise,' she whispered. 'And this part of the building is Nadia's own little domain. This is where she entertains her special clients, or where they entertain each other. Usually you can only get to this section by way of a door she keeps locked. The stairway is supposed to be a secret. I only found it by accident.'

Lianne could well believe that last statement, for they had accessed the stairs by way of what had appeared to be a small storeroom, at one end of which, behind several discarded rolls of carpet and a stack of cardboard cartons, Ellen had pulled aside a dusty velvet curtain to reveal the narrow doorway. There had been a key in the lock, but the mechanism itself was so corroded by age that it refused to turn either way, but it was stuck in the unlocked position and the handle had turned easily enough.

'What happens if we get caught down here?' Lianne demanded. Ellen shrugged.

'We'll probably get the same as Suzy's about to get,' she said. 'Plus a couple of hours on Jumbo, so it's not all that bad.' She stifled a giggle and tugged at Lianne's arm to indicate for her to follow. With a sigh of resignation Lianne began to move after her, wishing she had left the boots off and trying hard to put her feet down gently to prevent the heels from making too much noise.

Unlike Ellen, Lianne had changed after their brief

exchange of passion. She still wore the rubber stockings, but she had removed the restrictive corset and replaced it with a rubber suspender belt to keep her hose up. Over this she had selected a black latex mini dress with a slightly flared skirt, a high collar and short sleeves that just covered the tops of her gloves. She had intended removing the gloves, but Ellen had persuaded her to leave them on, saying they looked "cute" with the dress. Lianne was rapidly reaching the conclusion that Ellen was a total rubber fetishist, but then she told herself, when she looked at herself in the mirror, she wasn't so far off it herself.

She wore no brassiere under the dress, but the molded bodice gave her breasts all the support they needed, even if they did bounce alluringly when she walked. Somehow, Lianne found this made her feel extremely sexy, and she began to wonder what she would be like by the end of her first week in this place. Only twelve hours earlier she had been sitting down to a breakfast of toast and coffee wearing a sensible skirt and blouse and a pair of flat-heeled brogues, and now here she was creeping about a spookily huge house that was populated by a bunch of kinky sex orientated weirdos.

They didn't have far to go as it transpired. Ellen stopped after less than twenty paces and groped in the dark for a door handle. It turned with a faint squeak and the door swung noiselessly inward on well-oiled hinges. Ellen reached back for Lianne's hand and guided her into the room beyond, closing the door when they were both safely inside.

'What now?'

'Shhhh… Just wait a minute. I'm looking for something.' The room was even darker than the corridor, if that were possible, but suddenly Ellen pulled back a curtain and the place seemed flooded with light, though in reality the amount of illumination which penetrated the glass screen was very little. Lianne, however, was more taken up with the tableau that was revealed before them. As she stared through the glass Ellen put her face close to her ear and whispered urgently.

'It's a one way mirror. We can see them, but they can't see us. There's also an audio link, but don't make too much noise, because it's not completely soundproof in here. Come and sit down. There are plenty of seats, see?'

Lianne slipped into one of the seats immediately in front of the panel, hardly able to take her eyes off the scene in the other room. There were three of them there: Nadia, Suzy, and what was almost certainly Gavin, though he was wearing his leather hood again so it was impossible to be absolutely certain. Suzy was still wearing her catsuit and helmet mask, complete with the corset and boots. But Nadia had changed, and now strutted about, resplendent in a black leather corset and long gloves and thigh length black boots, on the heels of which jangled a pair of vicious looking spurs. She wore a heavy collar about her throat, very similar to the one Carla had worn in the other cellar and, in one hand, she carried a long riding crop, which she was brandishing in the air and swishing experimentally.

It was very clear exactly what she was going to do with the whip, for Suzy had been stretched over something that looked not unlike a pommel horse, her wrists and ankles fettered to the four legs, her broad rump jutting upwards to make a perfect target.

Ellen reached forward. There was a click, and from

speakers above their heads came the sound of Nadia's voice, not very loud, but perfectly audible.

'—ungrateful little bitch,' she was saying to Suzy. 'I pay you a perfectly good salary, you get all your expenses paid, and I've even agreed you can bring any of your little dyke friends to stay – but that's not good enough for you.'

'But the last time I brought a friend here she ended up moving in with one of your precious models,' Suzy wailed. 'It's not fair, madame, I can't compete with them. It's not my fault I can't lose weight and I'm too short.'

'So you dress up like a fat little snake and take advantage of a poor defenceless girl who hasn't been with us for five minutes. We lost two girls earlier this year because of you.'

'At least I didn't stick a cock in her mouth.'

'Only because you don't have one, I suspect,' Nadia sneered and, without warning, dealt Suzy a vicious backhanded swipe across her backside. The sound of the leather crop on the taut rubber was like a gunshot in the confined space and Lianne jumped with alarm. She opened her mouth, but before she had the chance to make a sound Ellen had her hand over it, making quiet shushing noises in her ear. In the next room, however, Suzy was much more voluble, letting out a shriek of pain. Nadia walked around the helpless girl, tapping her lightly with the end of the crop as if to emphasise her words.

'You,' she said, 'are a selfish, greedy, thoughtless little tart and you deserve a good thrashing. However, as I suspect you tend to enjoy being whipped, I have decided upon an alternative punishment – one that is more fitting for your crime.' Behind Suzy and out of her field of vision, Gavin had removed his boots and was now wriggling out of the tight leather trousers. Lianne saw that his cock was already half erect, but she was also bemused by the leather straps that encircled the base of his organ and the top of his scrotum. Leaning close to Ellen, she whispered a question into her ear.

'It's like an Arab ring,' Ellen replied, leaving Lianne none the wiser. Seeing this, she went on. 'What it does is delay ejaculation, or at least, it's supposed to. Also, when the man does come, it makes it really spurt. If you ever have sex with a man wearing one of those, you'll certainly feel the difference!'

Gavin was now naked apart from his cock harness, and was manipulating his shaft between his fingers, coaxing it into full and impressive life, though Suzy was still unaware of what was happening. Nadia continued her diatribe.

'Poor Lianne, who has only just arrived with us, was absolutely horrified at what you did to her,' she said. 'It just never occurs to you to find out a girl's particular leaning, does it? There are others here who are not at all averse to making love to another woman, especially Cindy.'

'But they all ignore me most of the time,' Suzy complained. 'Cindy thinks she's far too wonderful for the likes of me. I'm just here to do her hair and makeup and fetch and carry things, because they're all too high and mighty to do it themselves.'

'And so you pounce on someone who can't offer any resistance?'

'I wasn't the one who strapped her in the chair,' Suzy protested. 'It was just too tempting. I didn't mean anything by it, and I didn't hurt her.'

'No, you didn't hurt her,' Nadia agreed. 'At least, not physically. Which is why I don't intend to hurt you physically. However, I have decided it's time for you to find out what it feels like.' She looked at Gavin and nodded. He walked slowly around and stood in front of Suzy. She looked up and, seeing his now fully erect member, opened her eyes in horror. She strained her neck and stared up at Nadia, imploring her.

'Please, no,' she begged. 'Not that. Anything but that.'

'Oh, I'm afraid it has to be *that*,' Nadia sneered contemptuously. 'As I said, the punishment will fit the crime. Gavin is going to show you just what it's like to be screwed by someone of the opposite sex to that which you prefer.'

'But I never have done before,' Suzy sobbed. 'Not with a man, I mean.'

'I'm well aware of that,' Nadia said. 'And I am more considerate than you might think. Your vagina has never known a man's cock in it, and I do not intend to violate that sanctity now. However, there are other alternatives and I propose that Gavin shall explore them both.'

She stepped clear and Gavin closed in, aiming the tip of his cock towards Suzy's mouth. She, in turn, resolutely clamped her lips shut, but Nadia was having none of it.

'Open your mouth, you whore,' she commanded, 'or I shall rescind my earlier decision and Gavin will have your cunt as well. Not only that, but you'll stay on the horse all night and he'll have you in the morning, together with any of the other men in this house who might fancy a fuck with a fat little lesbian rubber lover. I think you might be surprised at how many takers we find.'

Her tone left little room for doubting that she meant

every word and, after only a second or two more, Suzy shut her eyes and opened her mouth. Gavin wasted no time on ceremony, immediately plunging the head of his phallus between the parted lips. For the first time since Ellen had pulled back the curtain, he spoke, his voice hard and unforgiving.

'Use your tongue, you bitch. Use it the way you do whenever you get your dirty little mouth on a nice juicy cunt.' Suzy made a series of grunts and mewling noises, but she had evidently complied with Gavin's instruction, for he said no more, simply standing there, gripping the sides of her latex sheathed head and steadily pumping in and out of her mouth.

Without realising it, Lianne moved her hand down between her own thighs and began worming her fingers inside the leg of her panties, where she was already wet once more.

'That's enough, Gavin,' Nadia said suddenly. 'Her mouth isn't deep enough to do that shaft full justice.' As he withdrew his glistening organ from between Suzy's lips, Lianne saw what Nadia meant, for the thick member had grown even more and, with its blue veins bulging under the semi-translucent flesh, was now at least ten inches in length. Lianne shuddered at the thought of what he was about to do with it, but as her fingers reached her clitoris the shuddering gave way to the first spasms of her own pleasure.

Slowly and deliberately Gavin moved around behind his victim, one hand trailing down her spine and tracing the cleft between her ample buttocks. He reached between her thighs and began fumbling with something, and Lianne remembered the crotch zip that ran from Suzy's lower stomach to a point level with the base of her spine, just two inches from where the main zip began its journey up her back to her neck. From the floor beneath the punishment horse Gavin picked up a pink coloured jar and quickly unscrewed the lid. Then, without any further ado, he quickly began lubricating her anal opening, thrusting one finger deep inside and bringing a gasp from Suzy's lips. Nadia relieved him of the jar and he moved in closer, repeating the careful aiming process he had used at the other end of the hapless girl.

As the hard tip began probing for the opening, Suzy let out a long shriek.

'Noooo...!' she wailed. 'Please, noooooo...!'

Gavin was unrelenting, but it became obvious that Suzy was fighting to resist him with her sphincter muscles, for Nadia closed in on her head again and raised her chin in one hand.

'You can stay here all night, remember,' she said. 'And we can leave you plugged with a rubber cock so fat you'll be easy meat for the morning.' Suzy sobbed, but the warning had had its effect. From the angle at which Lianne and Ellen were observing the spectacle they could not actually see the tip of Gavin's cock, but it became obvious when he finally affected a breech of Suzy's defences, for an inch or two disappeared from their sight. He was in no rush, simply standing there allowing the girl to get used to the feel of him inside her. Suzy groaned and gasped in a lungful of air, reopening her eyes, which were now wide and round behind her mask. Her mouth, too, formed an almost perfect circle as she awaited the inevitable.

It came in the form of one long deliberate thrust. Gavin's tethered balls disappeared between Suzy's cheeks as he impaled her with his full length. Suzy's shoulders bucked as far as her bonds would allow and she let out a long, banshee-like screech. At that very moment Lianne came, and for the next twenty seconds or so she was hardly aware of the adjacent performance.

As she finally began to regain control of her shivering body she noticed two things. Firstly, Gavin was now fucking Suzy with slow, languid ease and Suzy was beginning to pant like a dog in a heatwave. Secondly, in the seat next to her Ellen was completely engrossed in frigging herself through the now opened crotch flap in her catsuit.

Lianne wished she had brought her watch with her, for despite Suzy's initial protests and pleadings it was becoming increasingly obvious that Gavin's attentions were going to make her come, and Lianne would have bet that it would be in less than a minute. The problem was, without a timepiece it would be impossible to be absolutely accurate for when she came face to face with Suzy again.

CHAPTER SEVEN

'I still can't quite believe it!' Lianne exclaimed, throwing herself down onto the bed and grabbing her handbag to search for a cigarette. Ellen, who had perched herself on the stool and was busily unthreading the long laces of her boots, looked at her and grinned.

'If you're worried about Suzy, don't be,' she said. 'By the end there she was enjoying it as much as Gavin. I reckon she's just found out what she's been missing all this time.' Lianne extracted a cigarette from the rapidly depleting packet and flicked her lighter into flame.

'It wasn't Suzy I was worried about,' she confessed, exhaling a stream of smoke, 'it was me. How could I have done that in front of you?'

'Oh, I wasn't bothered,' Ellen assured her. 'I was too busy on my own account.'

'I know, but—'

'But now you feel embarrassed, or ashamed, or both?'

'Yes, I feel terrible about it all,' Lianne replied. 'I don't know what came over me. In fact, I don't know what's come over me altogether since this afternoon.'

'Oh, that's easy,' Ellen retorted, easing her foot out of the first boot. 'You just allowed yourself to let go and react at a very basic level, same as the rest of us do. It all seems perfectly natural when you think about it. Let's face it, this is hardly a convent and we ain't no nuns, baby. We earn our living providing diversionary entertainment for a section of the great unwashed, which is a lot bigger than you might think, so why shouldn't we get turned on by it as well? I mean, they only get to see the pictures, whereas we're actually here, involved in the original article.'

'Talking of which,' Lianne said, diverting the course of the discussion, 'why do they pay James to draw pictures from the photographs Simon takes? Why not just use the photographs?'

'Censorship,' Ellen replied, starting on the second boot. 'Drawings, sketches and paintings are considered art and no one dares censure art, whereas photographs are strictly regulated as to what they depict.'

Lianne snorted. 'Art?' she said. 'They class this as art?'

Ellen nodded. 'I think you should take a look at James' work before you start passing judgement,' she suggested. 'If you want to see some samples, look in the bottom drawer over there. They're only photocopies, but you'll see what I mean.'

When she pulled the sheets out of the heavy manila envelope, Lianne certainly did see and, having gone through the collection once, began again, only this time studying each black and white in greater detail. She was agog at the terrific atmosphere, tension, and expectation that the artist had managed to inject into each illustration. Not only had he managed to capture every nuance of light reflecting from rubber and leather, the suffering expressions on the victims' faces and the barely concealed malicious delight on the faces of their captors, but he had somehow managed to add an element that no camera could ever hope to capture, nor any photograph duplicate. Lianne was not quite sure what that element was, but as she came to the end of the portfolio for the second time, she just knew it was there.

'So, what do you think now?' Ellen asked. She had removed the boots, but had made no attempt to loosen her corset or take off her catsuit. Lianne selected one of the folios at random. It depicted a female captive shrouded from the neck down in gleaming white rubber, spread-eagled on a latticework frame by leather restraints. She was unable even to move her head, for her hair had been bound up into a high plait, leather thongs woven in with the hair and the extended braid stretched up to a ring high on the top of the frame. That girl was very obviously Ellen, even allowing for the macabre makeup and the undoubted licence of the artist in his depiction.

'That looks uncomfortable,' Lianne commented. Ellen lay back on the bed and reached out to take the drawing from her.

'It wasn't that bad,' she said. 'There were so many straps that my weight was distributed easily enough. The hair thing was a bit restricting, though. What you can't see from this is that Gavin had slipped a vibrator inside me and left it switched on through the entire session. Even Nadia didn't know about that, and she couldn't understand what I was making all the fuss about. That gag is inflatable and the great sod kept it fully pumped up so I could hardly make a sound.'

'Gavin seems to do just about anything he wants,' Lianne commented. 'Is there something going on between him and Nadia?'

'Good heavens no!' Ellen exclaimed. 'Nothing intimate, anyway. Nadia prefers her men a lot more submissive than Gavin, though I'm pretty sure she does take advantage of him if there's no one more suitable around at the time. No, Gavin just happens to be very good at his job. He's a natural dominant and he doesn't like women very much. Of course, he daren't go too far, not with Nadia around, but he pushes things to the sort of limits he knows she'll tolerate. For instance, he wouldn't dare actually inflict any physical damage on any of us – that would finish him here, but he uses snide little tactics like that vibrator, or for instance, things like leaving nipple clamps on for far too long afterwards. It was his idea to leave you on Jumbo, though Nadia insisted he switched it off.'

'But why the chair in the first place?'

Ellen laughed. 'It's a sort of tradition thing,' she said, 'like an initiation test. We've all been through it.

Personally, I don't mind it at all — not now. I can take Jumbo with no trouble. Actually, there's a second dildo that can be mounted just behind Jumbo. It's not so long, nor so thick, so you can guess where it goes. We call it Dumbo because it's not so big.'

Despite herself, Lianne was curious. 'What's it like — you know, with both of them?'

'You'd have to experience it for yourself,' Ellen replied. 'I can't really describe it, but let's just say it's a bit out of this world, especially the first time.' She rolled over onto her stomach, cupping her chin in one hand. 'If you want,' she said, 'we can go downstairs and you can try it. Nadia won't mind.'

Lianne shook her head and began peeling off one of the gloves. 'I don't think so,' she said, 'not after the day I've had. I'm too exhausted to move another inch.' Ellen rolled onto her back again.

'Fair enough,' she said. 'I must admit I'm feeling pretty bushed myself. Maybe tomorrow night, eh?'

CHAPTER EIGHT

The two girls were awake early the next morning, despite their exertions of the day before. Their first task was to strip off their rubberwear and take a bath. Ellen had made no attempt to remove her costume, other than the boots, and had also made no attempt to help Lianne out of her corset, so Lianne had resigned herself to copying her friend's example and sleeping cosseted in latex. The result was that two very sweaty females climbed into the large old-fashioned bath located in the room adjoining their bedroom and sank gratefully into the warm soapy water.

Lianne wanted to wash her hair, but Ellen cautioned against it, saying that Suzy was quite likely to be unavailable to redo it. They would also have to repair their own makeup, but Ellen assured her that she had had plenty of experience of that in the past.

'Just lie back and relax for now,' she said. 'I have a feeling this could be a long, hard day. Paul was on about doing some different scenes to what was originally planned. Apparently, he's quite taken with you and reckons you've got a bit of something over Stacey.'

'You do surprise me,' Lianne said. 'All yesterday afternoon I got the impression he was laughing at me. I think he's as bad as Gavin, in his own way. All this is just a good excuse to have a load of females tied up in knots.'

'Paul's all right,' Ellen said. 'He's a leather and rubber freak and he does love his bondage kick, I'll admit, but he's very imaginative and quite a softie, when you get to know him.'

'Sounds like you fancy him,' Lianne smiled.

'Not me, though I wouldn't be averse. Actually, I have done it with him, once when we had a bit of a party and we were both a bit pissed. He was quite good, though I was about as much use as a chocolate fireguard after the best part of a bottle of brandy.'

When they had towelled themselves dry and returned to the bedroom, Ellen set about the task of finding the items they were supposed to be wearing. Apparently Nadia had given her instructions as to what was required, but it still took her a little while to sort out the jumble of black leather and rubber. Lianne was concerned about what they should do with the soiled clothing they had worn for so long.

'Oh, that just stays in the bathroom. There's a couple of maids who are responsible for collecting it and getting it cleaned. It all has to be done by hand of course. The thin latex can easily rip if you don't treat it gently.'

As before, Ellen decided to dress Lianne first, having first spent fifteen minutes on her makeup. The first item was a long sleeved, high necked rubber leotard, again in black, but with an oval opening at the crotch which left her sex looking incredibly exposed. As with Ellen's catsuit, the sleeves ended in gloves, though this time they were fingerless and Ellen then proceeded to glue a set of incredibly long, bright red false nails over Lianne's own. She flexed her fingers, which now looked like an eagle's talons that had just been dipped in blood.

'I won't be able to do anything with these on,' Lianne complained. Ellen shrugged.

'You won't be expected to,' she said. 'And I won't need any help getting into my costume for today, so don't worry about it.'

Over the leotard went a thick rubber corset belt, almost identical to the one Ellen had worn the previous day, pulling in her waist savagely and emphasising her hips and her breasts where they were compressed inside their molded cups. Once again Lianne marvelled at the restricted feeling such a garment imposed upon its wearer. It made slouching impossible and sitting down a precise exercise.

There were no stockings this morning, just a curious pair of high-heeled boots that were more like a thigh length pair of strappy sandals, although the straps in question were made of thick rubber and there were six of them buckling about each leg between ankle and thigh. A vertical strap ran down the back of the leg, joining these horizontal ones and continuing up over the buttocks to join the waist belt. Even more amazing than the design itself, was the fact that every single buckle was lockable, though Ellen assured Lianne that one master key fitted all thirteen locks, including the belt. Another curious feature was that there was a strong steel ring set into the outside of every horizontal strap and another one on the inside of the ones which locked at the ankles.

When Ellen announced that there was also a mask with this outfit, Lianne was quite perplexed, for there was no way she could wear any sort of helmet without completely ruining her hair. However, this problem had been foreseen and cunningly solved by the designer. The mask, made from thick, very stiff rubber, was designed to cover only the lower half of the face, but with a molded extension that also covered the nose, ending in a tapering point between Lianne's eyebrows. It buckled and locked at the back of the neck and, when in place, followed the contours of her cheeks and jaws perfectly, though leaving just enough slack beneath the chin to enable Lianne to speak. A perfectly circular hole aligned with her mouth, but there were ominous looking buckles to either side of this and Lianne, who was rapidly beginning to learn what to expect, had little doubt that the aperture was there more to admit a gag than to enable her to talk.

She made her way slowly across to the mirror. 'Yikes!' she exclaimed. 'I look like some kind of android in this lot. All that's missing is the flashing red eyes.'

'Well, I can see one flashing red eye from where I'm standing,' Ellen commented. 'I forgot the crotch gusset.' She walked across to the wardrobe and began tossing things out onto the carpet, muttering under her breath as she searched for the missing item. After about a minute she gave a little cry of triumph and straightened up, waving a long thin triangular length in front of her. Lianne stood passively as her friend fixed the base end of the triangle to the bottom of her corset belt, buckling it at either end.

'Do you want a dildo in now,' Ellen asked, holding the thin free end of the strap, 'or would you rather wait till later? Gavin will have to do it again for the camera, I expect, but if you fancy it sooner rather than later, why wait?'

Lianne considered the offer, pursing her lips. Somehow, the straightforward manner in which Ellen had asked such an intimate question made her feel deliciously wicked. The Lianne of twenty-four hours earlier would have been horrified, but that Lianne was no longer present and she doubted whether she was ever likely to return. She took a deep breath and smiled, though the round hole in her mask prevented Ellen from seeing this.

'Now, I think,' she said quietly. 'And make it both, please.'

Ellen looked at her steadily, but her face betrayed no emotion or reaction. 'Your choice,' she said. 'But I choose the sizes – okay?'

CHAPTER NINE

The blonde woman stretched out one well-muscled arm and dropped the telephone receiver back onto its bedside table cradle. With her other hand she reached down and seized the coal-black hair of the head that was still busily at work between her massive thighs. The brown face emerged, mouth glistening, two huge dark eyes staring up at her without blinking.

'What is it?' she asked, pulling herself up into a kneeling position and drawing the brief, white satin nightdress back down over her hips. The blonde smiled at her, indulgently.

'I'm not in the mood any more,' she said, swinging her legs off the bed and drawing herself up to her full six feet three inches. She ran her hands through the stubbly silver brush which covered her head. Standing naked, she was an impressive sight, but she knew she was even more striking when she pulled on her favourite white leather. She fixed the Asian girl with a hard stare.

'He reckons it's time to make the first move, Marika,' she said. Her English was flawless, with only the merest hint of the singsong accent that betrayed the origins of most Scandinavians. 'Apparently they've got a new girl started, so any suspicion is likely to fall her way. In the meantime, I want you to get back on the phone and try to find us some decent new talent. That girl you brought in yesterday was totally hopeless. She fainted at the first sign of the whip, let alone the first stroke. Bloody

Barbara Schwartz and her agency – the woman needs a boot up her fucking arse!'

'I already phoned her, Christina,' Marika said. 'I told her you weren't very happy.'

'And what does Ms Schwartz propose to do about it?'

'She's trying to find suitable substitutes,' the darker girl said. 'Apparently, all her best girls are contracted out to some film director in the Bahamas.'

'Then look elsewhere,' Christina snapped. 'Get hold of Pieter in Rotterdam. He must have a few properly trained girls we can use.'

'Yes, but it's getting them into the country, isn't it? I mean, they're docile enough all the time they're kept under proper restraint, but the customs officers are hardly going to miss two girls in handcuffs and gags, are they?' Marika swung her own legs off the farther side of the bed and stood up, stretching her arms. At five feet eleven, she was a tall girl in her own right and only the presence of the amazonian Danish woman detracted from this fact. Christina began toying with the huge pink nipples that adorned her own massive breasts and let out a sign of exasperation.

'If necessary, get him to hire a boat. Pieter's got enough contacts in the smuggling business to run a couple of tarts past the British Customs and Excise.' She sighed again. 'It shouldn't be that hard to find the right people. Apparently Nadia's latest recruit is a bloody natural, once she got over her initial reserve. Why can't we find someone like that?'

'We had a far better choice in Hamburg,' Marika reminded her.

Christina snorted. 'Yes, but they were a load of cheap

whores. They all looked as though they hadn't slept in a year, or had a decent meal in two. They were all jaded. We need fresh faces – a typical English rose type, blonde and innocent. With all the money that's gone into setting up this place, I don't want to see it all wasted just because we can't find the right girls!'

CHAPTER TEN

To Lianne's surprise the day's shoot was starting in the open air, and she was a little reluctant to go outside the security of the house at first.

'What if someone sees us dressed like this?' she said. The two rubber phalluses had already started doing their work during the precarious descent from the upper floor, but the prospect of exposing herself to any old passers-by was a daunting one. Ellen took her hand and squeezed it.

'Remember the drive here?' she said. 'Remember the long lane before we got to the gates at the end of the main driveway? Well, you were probably too fogged with your vodka to have noticed it, but when we turned into the lane there was a big steel gate. That marks the edge of the estate, and it'll be locked now. Nadia's got nearly a hundred acres here and it's surrounded by a high security fence to keep poachers away from the grouse woods and prying eyes away from whatever else goes on here. There are also two gamekeepers who patrol the perimeter on a regular basis.'

'This game must pay more than I thought,' Lianne

replied. Ellen chuckled.

'It certainly pays a good whack,' she agreed, 'but Nadia doesn't need it any more than you need an extra hole in your head. She's already worth a packet. This lot was originally bought by her great grandfather, off the impoverished lord whose daughter he eventually married. Her grandfather inherited it from him and Nadia, who he brought up after her father died and her mother ran off with some Austrian bloke, got the lot when the old man died about ten years ago.

'There's also stocks and shares, several farms that are leased out, and a chain of shops that sell the sort of stuff we're wearing now, though they were founded by Nadia, rather than her granddaddy.'

'Then if she's that rich,' Lianne asked, 'why bother with all this in the first place?'

'Can't you guess?'

'Not immediately, no,' Lianne replied. Ellen squeezed her hand tighter.

'Listen, cuckoo,' she said, 'how do you feel right at this moment?' Lianne considered the question.

'Nervous,' she said eventually. 'Nervous and tense.'

'And?'

Lianne tensed her internal muscles, gripping the two rubber intruders. 'Excited,' she said quietly. 'Turned on, if you like.'

'Oh, I like, all right,' Ellen retorted. 'And so does Nadia. Nadia does this because she enjoys it and so does everybody else here. We may get paid as well, but I reckon most of us would still do it, even if there wasn't a nice little wedge at the end of it.'

'Oh, I see,' Lianne said – and she did, for as they stepped out onto the wide expanse of lawn and began

73

slowly crossing the lush grass, she was beginning to think that she, too, was possibly still here for motives other than monetary ones.

Progress in the tall boots was necessarily slow, even though Lianne had spent her time practicing in them whilst Ellen had dressed herself. The older girl was now attired in a far less revealing outfit than Lianne had anticipated. First, she had donned a long corset that covered her buttocks and extended to completely enclose her full breasts, though with cutouts through which her stiff nipples protruded like two swollen acorns.

Rubber stockings had been followed by knee-high boots with high heels, and then a pair of long rubber gloves. Over this had gone a full length, voluminous rubber gown, the hem of which brushed the ground when Ellen walked, despite the height of her heels. The billowing sleeves ended in tight wristbands and there was a high, stiff collar that buckled about the neck, but the rest of the dress was loose, like a black tent. There was also some sort of mask, but Ellen was still carrying that.

'What happens today?' Lianne asked when they were halfway across the lawn. Ellen shrugged.

'Who knows?' she said. 'I was just told what they wanted us to wear. The rest of it is down to Paul. He'll have briefed Gavin and Carla, and Simon will have a script copy so he can position his cameras, but the rest of it is a case of wait and see. I prefer it that way; it adds to the fun.'

'You would,' Lianne laughed, but privately she felt exactly the same way. There was an element of fear in not knowing what to expect next. But that fear was exciting and was adding an extra dimension to the mix of emotions that were threatening to overwhelm her already. Okay, she knew that she could stop it right there, go back to the house and get herself out of the bizarre costume, always assuming she could find the keys, but she also knew there was no way she was going to do that. She was making a willing sacrifice of herself at this stage, but sometime within the next few minutes her will would become unimportant and she would be a helpless victim in whatever scenario Paul Dean had wrenched from his curious imagination.

They reached the far side of the lawn, which was bordered by a high and neatly trimmed privett hedge, into which had been set a latticed portico covered with red and white roses. It was all so typically English country garden, Lianne thought, and yet here they were looking like refugees from a fantasy world.

A narrow path led through the orchard that lay beyond the hedge, the uneven ground presenting an additional challenge to their footwear. But they continued their sedate progress without mishap for a further hundred yards until they reached the far side and an ancient timbered barn structure, the doors of which stood wide open. Lianne saw that the gathering from the previous day had arrived ahead of them, although there was no sign of Paul Dean, nor of the second redhead who had not appeared until the assemblage in the lounge. Those that were there, however, were dressed exactly as they had been yesterday, though this time there was no idle chattering going on.

In Paul's absence James Naylor seemed to be in charge of things, with Nadia, resplendent in a brief red leather minidress, matching knee boots and a flowing red satin cape, content to sit on an upturned barrel and observe. In front of the open doorway, Carla and Gavin were bolting two heavy timbers together to form a large T-shape on the ground. Away to the left, Hazel was going through the contents of a large, brassbound trunk, arranging certain items on a trestle-table alongside it. With a small shudder, Lianne saw three different length whips, a long bamboo cane, and a thick leather strap into which had been set three rows of rounded metal studs. There were also several lengths of chain with leather manacles at either end and a flat board with three circular holes in it. Looking closer, Lianne saw that the board was in fact made in two halves, with a hinge at one end and a lock at the other. The centre hole, she saw, was large enough to encircle an average neck, the two outer holes clearly intended for the wearer's wrists.

Simon Prescott was mounting his final camera on its tripod to the right, the first two having already been set up centre and left. There was another trestle-table close to where he was working and on it lay two more smaller cameras and a collection of lens cases. There was also a leather case about two feet long and a foot square and a fourth tripod, still folded up, leaning against the table at one end.

At the sound of their approach, James Naylor turned to Lianne and Ellen and turned his arm to check his wristwatch.

'Kind of you to grace us with your presence, ladies,' he said churlishly. 'We've been waiting for you for the past fifteen minutes.' Ellen scowled back at him.

'I'd like to see you get into these costumes any quicker,' she snapped. 'Come to think of it, Jambo, you'd look quite cute in rubber stockings and a corset.' Naylor

76

returned her scowl and turned back to see how Gavin and Carla were progressing. Evidently satisfied, he returned his attention to the girls.

'You,' he said, stabbing a finger at Ellen, 'get over there and stand by the table. As soon as Simon's got a couple of shots of you, Hazel can put your mask on you. And you,' he pointed to Lianne in turn, 'just keep out of the way somewhere until we need you.' As Ellen started to move across to Hazel's table Lianne looked about for somewhere to sit. The only option was another barrel, next to the one already occupied by Nadia. The older woman, seeing Lianne's uncertainty, beckoned her over.

'Park your butt on the butt,' she invited when Lianne had joined her. 'You can smoke if you like.' Lianne pointedly looked down at her outfit.

'I'm afraid I didn't bring any cigarettes out with me,' she said. Nadia reached inside her cape and produced a silver cigarette case and a matching lighter. Lianne accepted them both, mumbled her thanks and, despite the handicap of her new talons, eventually managed to extricate one of the long filter-tipped tubes and get it alight. As she passed the case and lighter back to their owner, Nadia raised her eyebrows slightly.

'I take it you've not had any second thoughts?' she said. Lianne shook her head, exhaling a cloud of smoke.

'What would you have done today if I had?' she asked. Nadia shrugged.

'Probably used Suzy as a temporary stand-in,' she replied, 'or else taken the part myself.' Lianne stared at her.

'You?'

'And why not?' she said. 'Did you think I just liked

77

the dominant thing?'

'Well, yes, I suppose I did,' Lianne admitted. 'I didn't think—'

'You didn't think I could possibly allow myself to be chained up and treated like a sex object,' Nadia finished for her. 'Well, you know what they say about a change being as good as a rest. Anyway, you're still here, so the problem hasn't arisen, has it?'

They fell silent as Lianne drew on her cigarette, but eventually she could control her curiosity no longer.

'Where's Suzy today?' she asked. Nadia turned to her and winked.

'Somewhere she can't get at you,' she said. 'I've left her to dust and clean a total of twelve rooms. But to make it a more interesting punishment, she's wearing a locking harness with an inbuilt vibrator, the battery of which is good for at least three hours. I also locked her elbows to her corset and her wrists are joined by a chain. The ankle hobble won't make the job any easier, either.'

'Bloody hell,' Lianne said, before realising it. 'The poor thing will be half dead by the time she's finished.'

'Well, it'll certainly take care of some of her excess energy,' Nadia admitted. 'And it should do something for that libido of hers into the bargain.'

Lianne returned her attention to what was happening in front of the doors. Gavin and Carla had finished bolting the two lengths of timber together and were now threading straps through slots set at various intervals in the wood, their positioning making it very clear what they were intended for. With a deep sigh, Lianne guessed that before very long they would be strapping her down onto the T-shaped frame, but to her surprise it was Ellen who was summoned forward. She still had the mask clutched in her hands, but Hazel followed her as Simon clicked happily away.

'Okay, hold it there,' James called out when Ellen was close to the frame. 'You can put the mask on her now.'

Nadia held up a hand. 'I thought Paul's original script was for the mask to go on afterwards, when she's strapped down and lifted.' James shot her a venomous look.

'Her head will be at least seven feet up,' he snapped, 'and we don't appear to have a stepladder. Unless you want one of us to go back to the house, that is?' Nadia slowly stood up and took a pace away from the barrel on which she had been sitting.

'Use this,' she said quietly. 'I'm sure Gavin can climb up on it without too much trouble. He's a fit lad, as we all know.' Gavin grinned and Carla stifled a giggle with her hand. James glared about him and, for a moment, Lianne thought he was going to say something, but in the end all he did was shrug his shoulders.

'Suit yourself,' he said. 'I'm only the bloke who draws the pictures; what would I know?' Ellen turned her head, her eyes asking the question of Nadia, who nodded curtly. Passing the mask to Hazel, Ellen started forward again, camera shutters clicking at every step. As Gavin grasped Ellen's arm and began moving her into the position he wanted, Nadia crossed to the far camera and began pressing the shutter release. She looked up, caught Lianne's eye, and nodded to the remaining tripod.

'You get a few shots from there,' she said. 'It's all automatic, so all you need to do is press that green button on the top right. Give it about ten seconds between shots.'

Lianne obediently took up station on the centre camera

and peered into the large viewfinder. It gave a perfectly framed picture as Ellen was slowly lowered onto her back, laying along the upright of the T, her shoulders level with the crosspiece and her feet about thirty inches from the base. As Lianne began pressing the shutter release she saw for the first time that there was a rectangular hole in the ground a few inches from the bottom of the upright beam, and guessed immediately what it was for.

Meanwhile Carla and Gavin were busy securing Ellen to the frame, buckling the heavy straps about her ankles, thighs, waist and chest, crushing the fabric of the loose rubber dress tightly against her body as they worked. When the four main straps had been buckled they turned their attention to Ellen's arms. Drawing them out along the T they buckled three straps about each limb at ankle, elbow, and shoulder, so that she was now held to the frame as rigidly as if she had been a part of it.

Their task finished, Carla straightened up and stood back, but Gavin knelt above Ellen's head, leaned forward over her face and gently kissed her. Such a tender gesture shocked Lianne, who had already come to regard the big blond as something of a brute. As the couples' lips broke contact Gavin whispered something to Ellen. Lianne was too far away to make out his words, but she saw her friend smile up at him.

'Okay, if we're all ready,' James Naylor called, clapping his hands. Gavin and Carla took up positions; Gavin crouching at Ellen's head, Carla at the base of the frame, but Simon Prescott held up his hands to interrupt.

'Sorry folks,' he called. 'I forgot to set the video up for this. Just give me a minute, will you?' He moved across to where the spare tripod was and quickly erected it near to his original stills camera. From the case on the trestle-table he hefted a solid looking piece of electronic gadgetry and settled it atop the tripod, tightening butterfly nuts, peering through the viewfinder and making several fine adjustments. At last, pressing a switch on one side of the video camera, he stood back.

'Right, now we're running,' he announced. 'Sorry again for the delay. Carry on.'

Without further ado Gavin reached down, grasped the crosspiece of the frame, and lifted it and Ellen up to an angle of about forty-five degrees to the ground. Upon his nod, Carla took hold of the base and began dragging it towards the rectangular slot. As soon as she had it correctly positioned Gavin deftly changed his grip and continued raising the frame until the base end finally slid into the waiting hole. Hazel sprang forward, holding a wedge-shaped section of wood, thrust it into the space between timber and earth and stamped it home. Satisfied that the frame was well secured, Gavin stepped away and came around to one side. He looked up at Ellen as she hung just above him.

Lianne stared at her friend's face, but there was no sign of distress on her features, the straps apparently distributing her weight between them fairly comfortably. She presented a strangely erotic sight as she hung there, even though her body was swaddled in the crumpled folds of rubber, but there was inevitably more to come.

Dragging the empty barrel over so that it stood behind the helpless girl, Gavin, the shapeless rubber mask in his hand, stepped up onto it. Nadia motioned for Lianne to keep taking photographs as she was herself and, with Simon once more concentrating on his original camera, the air was full of clicking shutters as Gavin lifted the mask above Ellen's head.

There was no opening other than for the neck and Gavin was forced to stretch the latex to its limit in order to fit it over Ellen's skull. It clearly required quite an effort, yet when he finally pulled it down about her throat it didn't seem to be at all close fitting; hanging limply like a deflated balloon. Lianne realised that that was because it almost was a balloon; the baggy rubber being only the outer skin, the tight fitting part the inner. She saw there was a short tube extending from the back, on the end of which was a black bulb shaped like a small rugby ball. When Gavin began pressing it rapidly, air was forced in between the two layers of rubber and the mask quickly began to inflate.

Gavin finally let go of the bulb, and Ellen's head had become a featureless round ball with just a small aperture roughly where her nose had been. Lianne assumed this was to allow her friend to breathe. Heart thumping, Lianne wondered how Ellen must be feeling now, hidden away inside the grotesque mask, completely blind and probably unable to hear more than just an indistinct mass of background noise.

The cameras ceased their staccato harmony and now it was Lianne's turn. She allowed Gavin to lead her forward, and stood meekly whilst Hazel approached carrying two long steel rods. The reason for the rings in the straps of her weird and wonderful boots was now revealed as Hazel began passing the first rod down through them. Lianne saw that there was a flattened round disc on the top to prevent the rod from passing right through, but the rod seemed to be more than a foot too long, touching the ground long before the disc came into play.

However, when Hazel had finished threading the second rod in the same way the mystery was solved. Gavin stepped past Hazel clutching a business-like lump hammer. He kicked Lianne's legs apart as far as they would reasonably go without her overbalancing, and then proceeded to hammer on the top of each rod in turn, driving them into the ground until the discs were indeed touching the top ring on either side. Lianne looked down in amazement. It was a fairly crude concept but a very effective one, for with the rods driven so far into the ground it would take quite an effort to prise them out and, until she did, she was effectively stuck in this ungainly pose.

Carla, meanwhile, had brought the pillory board from the table and, with Hazel's assistance, expertly slotted it about Lianne's neck and wrists. Now she really was helpless, for even had she had the strength to extract the rods there was no way she could do so now. The two women stepped back and it was Gavin's turn again. He was holding what Lianne at first assumed was a short black dildo, but when she saw the straps hanging from its base she guessed its true purpose.

Presenting it to the round opening in her mask, Gavin pressed it home – Lianne dutifully opening her mouth to accommodate it – and quickly buckled the two little straps to prevent it from being ejected. He stood back again, grinning. All Lianne could do was stand there, lips stretched around the stubby cock, tongue pressed flat, as helpless as the day she was born and with considerably less options of sound or movement. She sighed, expelling the air through her nose, and wondered what on earth else they had in store for her.

She did not have to wait long for the answer. From the barn behind her a sinister black figure appeared, moving around in an arc until it came into her field of vision. The woman – Lianne could tell it was female only because it had large breasts thrusting against the molded cups in her catsuit – was encased in rubber from head to toe and stalked menacingly on thigh high boots whose heels mirrored Lianne's own. About her waist, over the latex skin, she wore a heavy leather corset with rows of spikes following the boning lines. From the bottom of the corset a triangular leather gusset, similarly spiked, disappeared between her thighs, re-emerging as a narrow strap between her buttocks. Her mask was contoured to resemble a face, the mouth-opening lined with red. The eye-openings were rimmed with the same colour, slanting upwards at the outer extremities to lend an oriental touch. As she drew closer, Lianne saw that each eye was covered by a green tinted lens, rendering the woman completely anonymous, though Lianne guessed she had to be the second redhead from the previous evening.

The woman circled Lianne slowly like a big cat in a circus ring, her studied movements sending delicious thrills of apprehension and anticipation running up and down Lianne's spine. Whatever the script called for her to do next, the cat woman was in no hurry, for she stopped directly in front of her intended victim and stood posing, hands on hips, legs slightly apart. To either side the cameras clicked and whirred, but not another sound disturbed the tranquility of the little clearing and Lianne sensed that a new tension had descended upon the little gathering.

Suddenly the woman parted her lips and let out a loud

hiss. Lianne responded with an involuntary gasp of surprise and would have stepped backwards, had her legs not been so thoroughly anchored. She saw the red lips within the red lips curl in an unmistakable smile as the woman closed in on her and, despite herself, Lianne let out a nervous little whimper. The smile broadened as hands reached out for Lianne's breasts. Rubber fingers grasped rubber orbs and Lianne groaned, closing her eyes. The hands began to squeeze and caress, lifting her breasts and molding them between strong fingers. Beneath the thin latex, Lianne's nipples stood out hard and prominent and she felt the walls of her vagina contracting spasmodically around the hard rubber cock.

However, if the object of the exercise was to make Lianne come, it was to do so eventually and not just yet. The hands left her and descended to search out the rear buckle of her crotch strap, which soon dropped down, hanging loosely over Lianne's sex. Fingers explored behind it, seizing the base of the front phallus and working it in and out. The ensuing spasm caused the rear plug to be ejected, shooting out onto the grass between her spread legs. Lianne groaned again, feeling the familiar warm tide beginning to gather, but still the cat woman denied her.

Releasing her hold on the dildo, she first loosened and removed the gag and then quickly unbuckled the front of the crotch strap and held it up, running the strip across Lianne's lips and letting her smell the evidence of her own excitement that had permeated it. The woman's tongue flicked out from between her lips in an unmistakable gesture. Obediently, Lianne used her own tongue, licking the heavy rubber and cleaning it of the little dribbles of her own juices.

Abruptly, the cat woman snatched the belt away, holding it aloft like a trophy. She twirled around, swishing the air with it, stepping backwards and flicking it towards Lianne's vulnerable sex. The thin tip cracked the air mere inches from the bare flesh. Lianne yelped in alarm. She heard several gasps from the onlookers, but she was beyond caring about their reactions, her gaze fixed upon those green eye slits as the woman continued to sway in front of her.

At last Lianne could stand it no longer. 'Please,' she gasped, 'do something – anything.' Her whole body was coming alive now, screaming for fulfillment, demanding satisfaction, but the cat woman remained unmoved. Again she flicked out with the strap and this time Lianne's cry was of pain, for the tip flicked against her tender flesh, sending a bolt of lightning searing through her body and only the steel rods prevented her from falling backwards. As it was, she slumped forward as far as the corset would allow, wishing she could free her hands to cover her intimacy. But as suddenly as it had been inflicted, the pain changed to a different sensation. She looked up, her eyes pleading silently with her tormentor.

The cat woman's posture was arrogant now, as though she knew she had her victim, as indeed she must have, but still she was playing with her, teasing and tormenting, making her wait, wanting her to beg. Lianne opened her mouth to do just that, but at the last moment some inner rebellion stopped her and she straightened herself, her chin lifting defiantly.

'Do it,' she hissed, not quite able to believe what she was saying. 'Do it, if you dare!' Again the smile and the woman stepped forward, grasped the base of the dildo and slid it from her. She forced Lianne's mouth open, and before Lianne could react the glistening rubber phallus was eased between her lips.

'Suck!' The order came as a hoarse whisper as the cat woman stood with one hand behind Lianne's head, and the other keeping the cock in place. Obediently, Lianne began to suck, tasting her juices even more strongly than she had done from the strap. Cat woman nodded, satisfied, but did not withdraw the shaft for what seemed like an eternity. When she finally did she stepped back and held it aloft for the cameras to see the evidence of Lianne's efforts. Someone started to applaud, but was quickly shushed by others. Lianne licked her lips, swallowing hard. Her heart was thumping like a machine gun now, her sex screaming at her brain. She tried to speak, but the words would not form themselves properly.

The cat woman tossed the black cock towards Gavin, who caught it effortlessly in one hand. She then stooped to retrieve the crotch strap and moved behind Lianne.

Crack! The rubber exploded across Lianne's buttocks and she squealed, more in surprise than pain.

Crack! *Crack*!! Twice more the strap laced across her flesh. Her upper body swayed back and forth like a demented marionette, but the cat woman was back in front of her again, the strap gone. She clapped her hands and Hazel stepped forward, handing her something that glinted. She took it, and obscured its identity from Lianne as she closed in again.

Rubber fingers delved between Lianne's thighs, probing between the wet lips and fingering her with surprising gentleness. They moved upwards, pressing against her clitoris, dragging yet another moan from

87

Lianne. But the groan was immediately replaced by a sharp cry, for the fingers suddenly grasped her pubic hair and jerked. Lianne tried to give with the pull, but the boots and their unyielding rods made it impossible. She was forced to stand there, enduring the dull pain. Tears filled her eyes, blurring her vision, but when the pull suddenly relented she did not need to see what the woman held up to know that she had cut off the hair with the scissors she had been concealing in her left hand.

The process was repeated a second time, a third time, and a fourth time. Lianne wanted to cry out, to tell her to stop, but her pride would not let her. It didn't matter anyway, she told herself, for there was no way the woman would stop now, even if she begged her.

At last the woman was finished. Lianne forced a smile.

'Satisfied now?' she asked, fighting to keep the tremor out of her voice. Slowly, the cat woman shook her head. She turned to where Hazel was waiting once again by her table and nodded, barely perceptibly. Hazel half turned and lifted a tray, upon which was a metal basin and several other small implements. She presented it to the cat woman. Lianne looked down and her stomach did a little somersault as she saw the brush and the safety razor and the small can of shaving foam that stood next to the basin of water.

'She's going to shave the nasty stubble off your little quim, Marylou,' Hazel whispered, blowing a tiny kiss towards Lianne. 'Then we'll all be able to see that sweet little cunny when she fucks you.'

The cat woman worked with ruthless efficiency. The shaving brush was really superfluous, given the creamy lather that the can supplied, but she used the bristles to good effect, deliberately working them between Lianne's swollen labia and on down into the groove of her bottom. Lianne was dimly aware that Simon Prescott was on his knees, barely a yard from them, his hand held camera recording every razor stroke in intimate close up. As the blade sliced through the foam, Lianne tensed herself, hardly daring to breathe as the steel edge was dragged to the very edge of her sex, certain that it would cut her most tender parts to ribbons. The hand on the razor, however, made no mistake, and in a very short while Lianne was left completely depilated, the air feeling strangely cool on her newly exposed mound. Hazel produced a damp cloth and gently wiped away the last traces of foam, the cold touch causing Lianne to draw a sharp intake of breath. When Hazel had finished, the cat woman stepped forward again, spreading her hand and covering Lianne's vulva and vaginal opening in an unmistakably possessive gesture. Now the rubber hand felt warm against her and Lianne closed her eyes in desperation.

'Please,' she groaned, 'let me come before I go mad.' Slowly, the hand released its grip and its owner retreated, standing and watching with hands on hips. 'Please,' Lianne repeated. The inscrutable smile said everything and Lianne knew she had been conquered, her body's needs betraying her. There was only one thing she needed now and they both knew it. The entire gathering knew it, too. She craned her neck, her eyes seeking Gavin, but the blond giant made no move towards her. Instead, with calculated deliberation, the cat woman began unbuckling the first of the straps that held her crotch strap in place. Lianne's eyes narrowed, watching her warily.

The fingers moved to the second strap, working it free of the buckle, but holding the spiked triangle in position. Then, slowly, she lowered it and Lianne let out a gasp of disbelief as a semi-erect penis and swollen balls were finally revealed. It wasn't possible, she told herself, but she knew that it was. Anything was possible here; even a voluptuous redhead being really a man. And that man's manhood was now quickly responding to his hands, swelling into an impressive erection that Lianne knew was intended for only one purpose.

The anonymous figure moved close again, waving the stiffening cock before him like a rapier. He stopped, inches from Lianne, who had to raise her head to look up into those featureless green eyes. Behind the mask the lips pursed in a mocking kiss and the rubber-sheathed breasts heaved in time with his breathing. Lianne's own chest felt as though it were about to burst, the teasing driving her insane with desire. She tried to peer down, but the pillory board blocked her view of his cock and it was only when he shuffled forward again, pressing the swollen tip against her wet lips, that she knew he really was now fully aroused.

The transexual figure remained perfectly and enigmatically still, apart from the gentle massaging of Lianne's opening with its thick shaft, as if it were waiting for some sort of signal. The clearing was now in total silence, even the cameras having fallen silent. Lianne wanted to turn her head to see the faces of the onlookers, but somehow she could not tear her eyes away from that macabre, masked face. As though in a dream, she saw the lips moving.

'Beg again,' they hissed. Lianne's mouth dropped

open, for this time the voice was not a whisper, nor was it in any way feminine.

'Paul?' she squeaked. The lips curled again.

'I said beg for it,' Paul Dean's voice came again, hard and unsympathetic. Lianne just gawped moronically. A hand closed about her right breast, squeezing painfully. 'Last chance,' he rasped, fingering her nipple. Lianne heard a voice in the distance, echoing somewhere in the clouds. It was her own.

'Please,' she cried, 'please fuck me!' As the distended helmet breached defences rendered virtually useless by her flowing juices, Lianne let out a little cry of triumph. As Paul Dean, alias the cat woman, buried his full length into her eager purse, Lianne's scream of sheer delight sent flocks of startled birds screeching from the surrounding treetops.

CHAPTER ELEVEN

Gavin and Carla had to carry Lianne between them when they finally released her. Inside the barn was a rubber-covered mattress set on a rustic wooden frame. They laid her on it to recover, and then went back outside to return their attentions to Ellen, who had remained strapped to the T-frame throughout. Left alone, Lianne tried to sit up, but the effort was too much for her and she fell back exhausted and trembling. Her fingers strayed to her sex, the rubber sliding over the wet flesh, and she smiled weakly, tears meandering down her cheeks.

She must have dozed, for when she next opened her eyes Ellen was bending over her, a slight look of concern on her features.

'You okay?' she whispered. Lianne nodded.

'Never better,' she replied. 'Totally knackered, but never better.' She struggled to sit up again and this time she managed it, thanks largely to Ellen's assistance. 'My legs feel like jelly,' she confessed. 'He screwed the life out of me.' She looked up at her friend. 'Did you know what was going to happen?' she demanded.

'No, I told you, I just had the details of what we were to wear,' Ellen reminded her. 'Come to that, I still don't know what did happen. I couldn't see anything with that mask on and all I heard was you screaming – at least, I presume it was you.'

'It was,' Lianne confirmed. Her voice still quavering, she outlined the events to Ellen. 'What is Paul,' she asked when she had finished, 'some sort of transvestite?'

Ellen perched herself on the edge of the mattress and put her arm around Lianne's shoulder.

'Paul Dean is an enigma,' she said. 'If anyone understands him at all, then it's Nadia, but even she reckons he's got her beat. He acts like a misogynist most of the time, and yet he'll happily dress up the way you described today.'

'Those boobs looked real,' Lianne said. 'They even bounced when he moved, and his hips didn't look masculine at all.'

'Padding,' Ellen explained. 'And the tits are made of the same sort of stuff that breast implants are made from. They cost a small fortune, from what I've been told.'

'But what does he get out of it?'

'Search me,' Ellen said. 'Like I said, the man's an enigma, a screwball even, though he's a genius at his chosen trade. His mind is so perverse and inventive, you wouldn't believe it.'

'Wouldn't I?' Lianne retorted. 'I think I would. You could have knocked me down with a feather when I realised it wasn't a woman. Up till that point I'd assumed the cat woman was that other redhead – not Hazel, but the one who was there last night.'

'That'd be Cindy – Cindy Fletcher. No, Cindy had to go into town today. She had a dentist's appointment, or something.'

'Well I know it wasn't her now, don't I?' Lianne grinned. She shook her head, looking down at her feet, still clad in the strappy boots. 'I'm getting worse, aren't I?' she said, her voice barely above a whisper. Ellen made no reply, waiting for her to amplify the question. After several seconds' consideration, Lianne looked up again.

'What's happening to me?' she asked. 'Is it this place? The clothes? The bondage stuff? I mean, two days ago you were having to go all out to persuade me to even come here, and that was before I realised the half of what was entailed. And yet now, I'm sitting here, looking like I don't know what, calmly discussing the fact that I've just been screwed to oblivion by a weirdo in a woman's catsuit, whilst staked out with my legs spread like a cheap whore.'

'Never cheap, darling,' Ellen enthused, giving Lianne a reassuring hug. 'You're priceless.'

'So now we've agreed what I am and we're just haggling over the price, is that it? I ought to feel so really ashamed of myself.'

93

'And do you?'

There was a short silence that felt like forever, before Lianne finally answered. 'No,' she said, 'I don't. At least, I don't think I do. If I did, I wouldn't be wishing I could do it all over again.'

'With Paul, you mean?'

'I'm not sure it would matter that much. I mean, he's good-looking and there's something about him, but none of that played any part in what happened out there just now. Let's be honest about it, I didn't even realise it was a man until the last thing and I was still begging for it. Anything would have done – a rubber cock, a vibrator, a finger! All I knew was that I desperately needed to come!'

'And Paul finally obliged, I take it?'

'Oh, I came all right. I thought yesterday was the best it could get, but today was out of this world. I think my brain just blew up.'

'So, you're still glad I talked you into coming?' Ellen said with a wry smile. 'No pun intended,' she added hastily. Lianne's eyes crinkled in amusement.

'What do you think?' she replied.

'I think,' Ellen said, 'that so-called civilisation has given us a distorted view of sex.'

The two girls were walking along a rough trail through thick woods on the eastern side of the estate. The afternoon shoot had been called to a premature halt when Simon Prescott started complaining that he was getting a migraine. James Naylor had suggested that he could take over as cameraman, but Nadia would hear none of it.

'You'll be looking at every shot from the point of view

of an artist,' she had explained, gently but firmly. 'It's much better when you work from Simon's prints. I don't know why, but the extra layer of detachment seems to make all the difference.'

Lianne and Ellen had returned to the house, stripped, showered, and selected a change of clothing. Ellen had opted for a pair of white leather hotpants, together with a white kid crop-top and matching ankle boots. Lianne had stuck with the latex minidress she had worn when they had spied on Suzy's punishment, but had left off the gloves and stockings. Her boots were knee high, her legs between their tops and the hem of her flared skirt left bare. It felt strange to be so unrestricted now, but the fresh evening air about her thighs and arms felt good.

'I'm beginning to see what you mean,' she said in response to Ellen's declaration. 'Though we could just be making excuses for ourselves.'

'So what?' Ellen retorted. 'Anyway, I'm way past needing an excuse, and you're catching up fast.'

'How long have you actually been doing this job?' Lianne asked, kicking a loose stone, which clattered against the trunk of a gnarled tree. Ellen pursed her lips in concentration.

'Over a year now,' she said. 'More like eighteen months, in fact. I know I've already built up a nice little nest egg.'

'And can you see yourself still doing the same thing in another five years or so?'

Ellen turned to Lianne, her eyes sparkling. 'I certainly hope so,' she said. 'I'd like to carry on for as long as I can. If I wear as well as Nadia has I could have another twenty years left in me, though I may have changed my mind by then and decided to settle down.'

'You haven't met your ideal man yet, then?'

'Depends what you mean by ideal,' Ellen said. 'There was a bloke, about two years back, but he decided to go and work with refugees in some really smelly part of the world – or that's what he told me. I got a couple of letters and started to feel guilty about not going with him, so I booked a flight out to some Bonga-Bongaland airport and spent another day and a half in this bus that was so ancient it had an outside loo. When I finally got there, guess what? My knight in shining armour was shacked up with this big-titted Irish nurse. I walked in right in the middle of her playing Grand National jockeys on top of him.'

'So what did you do?'

'What did I do? What could I do? I could have picked up a tent pole and rammed it right where the sun doesn't shine, but it wouldn't have done me any good, so I just walked up, slapped her on her big fat arse and walked out again. She got such a shock, but it was nothing to the look on his face. The pair had been at it so hard they hadn't even heard me come in. I laughed all the way back in the bus and cried all the way back in the aeroplane. Then I went out and got good and drunk, picked up the first fella I fancied, and took him back to my place.

'He was even more pissed than I was, so it didn't take long to persuade him to try a few kinky games. When I had him tied down on the bed I found this garden cane that had been holding up the rubber plant that had died whilst I was away playing safari's and started beating the hell out of his arse. And guess what?'

'He liked it?'

'He bloody loved it. He came all over my clean duvet cover, so I made him lick it up.'

'But that's a bit different from all this?' Lianne pointed out. 'Quite a reversal of roles, in fact.'

'I know, but that's a long story. My one-night-stand didn't do much for me. So I just went out again the next night and got drunk all over. Then this girl started chatting me up and I started pouring my heart out. She seemed sympathetic and she seemed to understand. Well, if I tell you her name was Hazel O'Dee, I don't think I need to say more, do I?'

'And she got you into all this?'

'She got me into a load of things, believe me. She's into fetish clubs and parties and she started taking me along with her. It was great, especially since I could wear a mask and nobody would have a clue who I was. Then, one night, there was this Mistress and Slave do. Hazel had to be the Mistress, naturally, so poor little me goes along with her wrists handcuffed behind her back, looking all sweet and helpless. Before I know what's happening Hazel pops a gag in my mouth and passes me over to this girlfriend of hers, who just happens to be very tall, very black, and very beautiful.'

'Carla?'

Ellen nodded. 'Uh-huh, you've got it in one. Anyway, I got one hell of an education that night, the following night, and the night after that. They took me back to this flat – it was Carla's, I think – and kept me as their slave for a long weekend. They'd have let me go if I'd insisted, of course, but I didn't. I was having too much fun. Then they brought in this guy. I couldn't see his face because he was wearing a mask, but he had a gorgeous body and he knew how to turn a woman on. Anyway, after that it was a short step to this. I got what I enjoyed most and got a fat wage packet to boot. I haven't looked back since.'

'And yet you needed to share a flat?' Lianne asked. Ellen shrugged.

'I saw you putting the notice in the shop window,' she confessed. 'I don't know why, but I just got this funny sort of feeling about you.'

'You mean that I looked like the sort of girl who'd enjoy wearing rubber and being trussed up?'

'I wouldn't put it quite like that, but you had a certain look about your eyes. I'd seen that look at the clubs and parties a hundred times before, and the faces I saw it on usually had owners and were wearing chains and straps and being good little submissives.'

'Oh, wonderful,' Lianne said. 'Shall I just stick a sign on my head saying, "Chain Me"?'

Ellen linked her arm through Lianne's. 'No need, my sweet,' she laughed. 'Anyway, aren't you glad I could tell?'

They walked on for several more minutes, the light slowly failing as the sun dipped nearer the horizon somewhere beyond their leafy world. Lianne was beginning to appreciate just how extensive the grounds of the estate were, for they had already covered at least half a mile since leaving the house and there did not appear to be any immediate end to the woods. The birds were heralding the approaching night in a noisy variety of treetop choruses, and they even saw three squirrels jumping from branch to branch high above their heads. Lianne sighed contentedly.

'It really is beautiful here,' she said. 'It's so peaceful. I feel as though I never want to see a town again.'

'You needn't – not if you don't want to,' Ellen told her. 'Nadia would be quite happy for any of us to live-in permanently. Gavin, Hazel and Carla already do. Mind you, you'd be expected to earn your keep between shoots.'

'You mean—?' Lianne looked at her friend quizzically. Ellen nodded.

'It's no different from what we already do.'

'I don't know about that,' Lianne responded. 'Posing for pictures is one thing, even if it does go a bit over the top, but actually performing for complete strangers – no, I don't think I could.'

'No, I do know what you mean,' Ellen agreed. 'I did try it once, but the guy was horrible and I didn't enjoy it one little bit, even though I did come in the end.'

Lianne giggled. 'I don't believe this conversation,' she said. 'In fact this is all a bit surreal. Look at us – two girls done up like centrefolds on *Kinks Weekly*, walking arm in arm through the most gorgeous countryside and calmly discussing the fact that you couldn't stand some bloke who brought you off! There must have been something else in that bottle, besides brandy.'

The trees suddenly became less dense and they emerged into a large clearing, in the centre of which was a small, single storey building made of very ancient looking brick. It had one door, one window, and was overgrown with bushes and ivy on one side.

'What is this place?' Lianne asked.

'Nadia's solitary confinement cell,' Ellen said. 'She uses it for certain guests when her other facilities are in danger of getting crowded. Want to see inside?' The door was locked, but there was a key hidden behind a loose brick and Ellen quickly used it. Inside it was almost totally dark, but Ellen knew her way around and soon had a small hurricane lamp lit. By its light they picked their way past a table and two stools and opened another door that led to an inner, windowless chamber.

As Ellen lit a second lamp, Lianne peered about her. Someone had evidently gone to a lot of work in this room, recreating the atmosphere of a medieval dungeon and torture chamber. One end of the area was separated off by steel bars, into which a barred door was set, reminding Lianne of the jailhouses as they were depicted in western films. There was a pillory, a set of stocks, and a sinister looking rack, which had been made to look old, though its ropes and straps looked pretty new. In one corner stood a body-shaped cage of steel bands, hinged to open and fastened by means of two heavy padlocks. Lianne imagined being imprisoned inside it, unable to move, yet completely vulnerable to anyone who cared to take advantage of the situation.

All along one wall, hanging from a timber rack, was an array of chains, manacles, hoods, harnesses, whips, paddles and canes. There was also a long, narrow leather sack, the purpose of which Lianne could only too readily guess. She walked across to the rack, lifted down a leather head mask and turned it over in her hands. It was beautifully crafted, laced at the back and secured by an additional collar that could be locked. On an impulse, Lianne handed it to Ellen.

'Put it on,' she said. Ellen quickly obliged and Lianne laced the back together, drawing the soft leather tightly about her friend's head. She closed the collar and looked around, searching for a lock. She found several hanging in a neat row, their keys all in them. Selecting the nearest, she clicked it into place, removed the key and, lifting her skirt, slipped it inside the tight rubber panties. Ellen's eyes, from behind the mask, looked quizzical. Her lips, visible through the narrow mouth aperture, were slightly pursed.

'What now?' she asked. Lianne grinned.

'Maybe I should chain you up,' she suggested. 'Either way, you get to wear the mask till morning.'

'Oh, little Miss Dominant now, are we?' Ellen giggled. 'Well, mistress, what can your humble slave do for you?' Lianne walked back to the wall rack and began examining the various manacles and chains, but just as she had made her choice Ellen held up a hand and made a shushing noise. Lianne froze, leather harness dangling from her hands.

'What's up?' she hissed. Ellen shook her leather-sheathed head and held a finger over her lips. She inclined her head slightly, but then shook it.

'Give me the key to this thing,' she whispered, indicating the collar. 'I can't hear properly with this on.'

'Hear what?'

'Didn't you hear it?'

'What?' Lianne repeated urgently, not understanding.

'An engine,' Ellen said. 'A car engine. Now give me that key – quickly.' Lianne passed the key over, but she was still perplexed.

'What's wrong with hearing a car engine?' she said. 'I think I did hear it, though it was a long way away.'

'Not that far away,' Ellen persisted, fumbling to insert the key. 'Not if we both heard it inside this building, and one of us has got a layer of leather over her ears. Oh bugger it, you try.' She turned her back on Lianne, passing her the key.

'But where's the problem over an engine noise?'

Lianne asked. 'Noise travels a long way, especially in the country, and more especially at night.'

'Not that far,' Ellen said. 'The perimeter fence is less than fifty yards on through the trees, and beyond that is an old disused road – little more than a mud track with a bit of gravel on it, really.'

'Well, there you are then,' Lianne said. 'Obviously someone's using it.'

'But why? That road goes nowhere, except to some derelict watermill that hasn't been used or lived-in for most of this century. The place is falling down and totally dangerous. What's more, you can only get this far up the track by driving across a bridge that's in little better condition than the mill itself.'

'Maybe the driver didn't know it was dangerous,' Lianne reasoned, trying to turn the key in the padlock. 'Maybe he's just lost.'

'Except for one thing. Though the bridge is outside the perimeter fence, it's still on Nadia's land, and she had the bridge blocked off with a steel gate that's kept locked permanently. As far as I know the only key is in her office.'

'Perhaps it's Nadia herself then.'

'You must be joking. She's got more sense.'

'But I still don't see – oh, bugger!' Lianne stared down at the stump of key that remained between her thumb and forefinger, the rest of it being still in the lock. Ellen turned, saw what had happened, and muttered something under her breath. Lianne looked at her helplessly.

'I'm sorry,' she said. 'It just sort of snapped. Maybe one of the other keys will fit?' Ellen shook her head.

'No time,' she said. 'I'll just have to go as I am.'

'Go where?'

'Out there, in the woods. Look, someone's out beyond the fence with a car and I don't like it at all. There's a gate just along from here, and though it's kept locked, you never know. It could be intruders.'

'But why?'

'Who knows? Maybe it's poachers, or burglars trying to case the joint. Either way, Nadia wouldn't like strangers getting a look at what goes on around here. One look at any of us in our working gear and they'd know they were onto something the tabloids would pay handsomely for.' She pushed past Lianne and led the way back outside. It was very nearly dark now and the trees had taken on a sinister aspect, especially if they were hiding potential danger – as Ellen seemed to think.

The perimeter fence, as Ellen had said, was not very far beyond where the girls had come so far, the heavy steel mesh supported by concrete pillars some fifteen feet high. Beyond it there were just a few scattered trees and beyond those again was the track that Ellen had described, on the other side of which was rough, open scrubland. With Ellen taking the lead they made their way alongside the fence, picking their way with extreme care over the mounds of broken twigs and exposed roots. Suddenly Ellen held up her hand and dropped into a crouch. Lianne followed suit and eased her way up until she was stooping alongside her.

'What is it?'

Ellen extended her arm, finger pointing. 'Look,' she hissed. 'There it is.' Lianne peered in the direction indicated, her eyes struggling to identify anything in the gloom, but suddenly she saw it; a darker outline next to what seemed to be a large bush. It was a vehicle all right, but a small van, not a car.

'Can you see anyone?' Ellen whispered. Lianne shook her head.

'I can barely make out the van,' she said. 'Perhaps there's someone inside.'

'I can't see any sign of anyone anywhere else,' Ellen said. 'Unless the driver's already gone to ground. The gate's just up opposite where he's parked.'

'Perhaps they'll try to climb over the fence?'

'Perhaps, though I doubt it. That's razor wire along the top up there and there's two sensor wires as well. Anyone or anything touches them and it sounds an alarm back at the house. Round the other side of the estate there are cameras too. But Nadia's never bothered over this section; there's the river and a stretch of marsh to cross before you get this far.'

'Unless you come up the road,' Lianne said. Ellen nodded.

'Unless you come up the road,' she agreed. 'Which someone obviously has.'

'So what do we do now?' Lianne asked.

'We try to get up by the gate without being seen. I suggest we drop back into the trees a bit. We're too exposed out here. Come on, follow me.'

A few minutes later they were crouched in the middle of some bushes, peering through the trees towards the gate. It appeared to be locked still and there was no sign of anything, or anyone, moving. However, just as Lianne was about to open her mouth to comment on this, the door of the van opened and they saw a man's head emerging above the undergrowth that all but concealed the vehicle from their present vantage point. Instinctively the two girls ducked even lower, watching the shadowy form as it picked its way towards the gate.

'Do you recognise him?' Lianne whispered. Ellen shook her head.

'He's still too far away, and anyway, I wouldn't recognise my own mother in this light.'

'She certainly wouldn't recognise you,' Lianne retorted, thinking of the leather mask. Ellen was not amused.

'Ha-bloody-ha!' she hissed. 'Bloody comedienne now, aren't we? Just shut up and keep down. It looks like he's waiting for someone – whoever he is.'

The dark figure had reached the gate and was just standing there, one hand resting on the wire, his attitude suggesting that he was trying to peer through the trees inside the perimeter. Cautiously, Lianne turned her head, trying to see in the direction he was looking. There was a narrow track leading inwards from the gate that passed the girls' hiding place only five or six yards away. It wound into the trees and disappeared into the darkness, which was very nearly absolute now.

They heard the other figure approaching long before it came into view. Twigs cracked underfoot as it made its uncertain way. When they first saw it, the black silhouette appeared to be female, but Lianne was taking nothing for granted after her earlier encounter with Paul Dean. In fact, she thought as the figure drew level with them, it looked just like Paul had looked. It was dressed from head to toe in black rubber, wearing the same boots and a mask with lenses covering the eyes, but it was having trouble walking over the rutted and hardened earth in the high heels.

The gate was just far enough away for the girls not to be able to make out the muffled verbal exchange between the two mysterious figures. The new arrival clearly had the key, for after a few seconds and accompanied by a squeal of rusty metal, the gate swung inwards. More conversation followed and something passed between them; a small package that the rubber figure had been carrying beneath its arm. Lianne put her mouth close to where Ellen's ear was beneath the helmet.

'What's going on?'

Ellen turned, finger to her lips, and shrugged. The two figures by the gate were becoming more animated now and there was quite a bit of hand gesturing from both of them. The girls still could not make out what they were saying, but the one thing Lianne was now sure of was that they were both male, despite the feminine outline beneath the rubber bodysuit. Logically, the second person had to be Paul Dean, but there was something nagging at the back of her mind that she could not quite put her finger on.

Whatever disagreement had been taking place by the gate had evidently been resolved now, for the rubber-clad figure turned and began walking back the way it had come, the van driver close on its heels. The girls ducked low again as the two passed and stayed down until they had disappeared into the darkness for some time. It was Ellen who finally broke the silence.

'I don't know what this is all about,' she said, 'but I definitely don't like it.'

'Do you think we should follow them?' Lianne suggested. Ellen's eyes were two dull glimmers in a sea of blackness.

'They could be anywhere in these woods by now,' she pointed out. 'And if they are up to no good, which I would say is a fairly safe bet, they could get nasty if we just blunder into them.'

'So what do you suggest we do?'

'Go back the way we came. At least we're going away from the way they went and we should be able to get back to the house without any trouble.'

'And then what?'

'I don't know,' Ellen admitted. 'We should say something to Nadia, I suppose, but exactly what, I haven't a clue. After all, what have we seen? Someone wearing what looks like Paul's suit meeting up with a stranger out here and passing him something or other we couldn't see. It's not much to go on, is it?'

'I take it you're not convinced that was Paul?'

'I'm convinced it wasn't,' Ellen said. 'It was someone about the same height, give or take an inch, but that doesn't narrow it down much, except that I also know it wasn't female. Both those voices were masculine, and whoever was wearing that suit isn't used to the high heels.'

'Which lets out Paul, because he moved in them like he's had plenty of practice,' Lianne said, finally realising what it was that had been bothering her. 'Which leaves James, Gavin, or Simon,' she concluded. 'Unless there are other men up at the house – guests, perhaps?'

'I think there are two couples staying tonight,' Ellen said, 'but at least one of the men is out of the frame. Right now he'll be hanging by his wrists in Nadia's private dungeon, with Nadia and his girlfriend giving him the time of his life.'

'What about the other couple?'

'Friends of Nadia's. They come for long weekends from time to time. They usually just watch the shoots and indulge in a bit of dressing up. The woman – her name's Sandra – likes to take a small part. Paul usually writes her in, just to humour Nadia.'

'So, we've got four suspects,' Lianne said. Ellen gave a little snort of laughter.

'Before you start hunting for clues, Miss Marple, I'd like to suggest we get the hell out of here. Wherever those two went, they sure as hell aren't going to be there all night and I'd like to be as far away from here as possible before they come back.'

'Shouldn't we at least wait and see what happens when they do come back?' Lianne suggested. Ellen grasped her arm firmly and stood up, taking Lianne with her.

'No,' she said emphatically. 'We stick with Plan A and shift our butts out of here – now!'

CHAPTER TWELVE

The two girls made the return journey to the house without further event, and made their way upstairs to their room without seeing any of the other occupants. Ellen took an unopened bottle of brandy from the wardrobe and poured them both a stiff drink.

'I think we should have a quiet word with Nadia,' she said, passing one of the tumblers to Lianne. 'She'll be busy down below right now, I should think. But first thing in the morning we should see her and tell her what we know.'

'Which isn't a lot,' Lianne reminded her. Ellen nodded and took a healthy sip from her own drink.

'No, it's not, but we should still say something.

Whatever that was all about, it didn't look kosher and she's got a right to know about it. Besides, if someone's using the bridge and it collapses under them it'll mean police involvement. Nadia can change the gate lock, if nothing else. Meantime, I'm going to sneak down to the cellar and try to find something to cut the lock on this mask. There's usually a pair of bolt croppers kept there, just for emergencies like this.'

Lianne slept well despite everything, and was awake with the dawn next morning. She shook Ellen, who mumbled something and turned over without opening her eyes. Lianne looked down at her friend, checked the time with the small clock on the chest of drawers, and swung her feet to the floor.

Unlike her first night at the house, this time she had slept completely naked and her first task was to find something to slip on over her nudity whilst she went to the bathroom. A brief examination of the wardrobe yielded a long wrap around negligee made of thin red latex, and a further search revealed that there was nothing in the room that was not made from either rubber or leather. She slipped her arms into the loose sleeves, the rubber cool and soft against her warm skin, and tied the belt loosely about her waist.

The house was very quiet beyond the bedroom door. Early rising was not considered a virtue here, Lianne reflected, smiling to herself. She decided to take advantage of her head start and ran a deep bath, adding various oils which she found on one of the bathroom shelves. She sank into the water and let herself float in its warm embrace for a full half-hour, massaging herself lazily from time to time and occasionally running her fingers over her smooth mound, the sensation still a curious one.

Shaking herself out of her reverie, Lianne stepped out of the bath and pulled the plug, drying herself whilst the water drained away. When it had emptied she rinsed the bath, replaced the plug and refilled it ready for Ellen, who she finally awoke when she returned to the bedroom.

'What do we do about food?' she asked her friend. 'In the last thirty-six hours all I've had is a few sandwiches. Doesn't anyone cook around this place?'

'There's a live-in cook,' Ellen explained, 'but she's off on holiday this week, so we have to fend for ourselves. When I've bathed and changed we can go down to the kitchen. There's a massive fridge and a couple of freezers, so I'm sure we can rustle up something for breakfast.'

When Ellen finally returned from the bathroom the two girls spent half an hour selecting what they were going to wear for the morning. Apparently there was no shoot planned until the afternoon and Ellen had received no instructions as to their required costumes, so for the moment they were free to choose for themselves.

Lianne decided upon a change from rubber, opting for a brief leather skirt and a sleeveless jerkin top with a plunging neckline. There was a choice of leather brassiere's, but she opted to leave her breasts free beneath the top and did not bother with any panties either. The choice of footwear was extensive, though all the heels were high. Lianne chose a pair of thigh length boots, the tops of which stopped just short of the hem of her skirt. Standing in front of the mirror she nodded self-approvingly, for the various items went well together and made her look quite dominant, which was a pleasing change.

Ellen was soon resplendent in a clinging red rubber sheath dress with a high collar and long sleeves, and a pair of gleaming red patent court shoes.

The kitchen was a huge place, designed in an age when servants were considered a necessity and not a luxury by the classes lucky enough to be able to afford them. There was still a massive coal-fired range, but there was also an easy alternative in the shape of a very modern electric cooker. As Ellen had predicted, the fridge, which was big enough for two people to stand in if the shelves had been removed, offered a wide variety of food options. But they settled on a fry up of eggs, bacon, sausages, beans and mushrooms, together with toast and a pot of tea. The smell of the bacon as it sizzled under the grill made Lianne realise just how hungry she was, and they were soon tucking in with gusto.

They were just finishing and about to pour themselves a second cup of tea when Suzy burst in. Her face was flushed and she wore an expression that was both concern and excitement.

'Have you heard?' she gushed.

'Heard what?' Ellen demanded. 'We've heard nothing. You're the first person we've seen this morning.' Suzy plumped herself down on an empty chair and reached for the single half-slice of toast that was all that remained of the two breakfasts.

'Paul's gone,' she announced and bit into the toast. 'And he's taken everything with him,' she continued through a mouthful of charred bread.

'What do you mean, everything?' Ellen prompted.

Suzy swallowed the chewed toast noisily.

'All of James' drawings, all his sketches, and all of Simon's photographs – including the negatives,' she said. 'Nadia's going mental and James is livid.'

'Could that be—?' Lianne began, but stopped short when Ellen kicked her ankle under the table.

'How do they know Paul took the stuff?' Ellen demanded. Suzy made to take another bite but stopped, the half-demolished slice inches from her mouth.

'Well, who else could it have been?' she said. 'Cindy saw him crossing the lawn last night, and he was carrying some sort of a case.'

'I presume he was still wearing that suit of his?' Ellen suggested blandly. 'The one with the padding that makes him look like a woman?'

'Yeah, he was. Cindy was looking out of her window and she reckoned he looked in a hurry – kept stumbling and all that. Anyway, that's the last anyone's seen or heard of him. It looks like weeks of work have gone west. James is threatening to dismember him if he ever catches up with him.'

'I can imagine,' Ellen said, flashing a warning glance at Lianne. They left Suzy refilling the frying pan with an entire packet of beef sausages and went back upstairs, neither of them saying a word until they were safely in their room with the door closed.

'I don't believe it,' Ellen said, walking over to the window and looking out towards the woods where they had witnessed the sinister rendezvous the evening before. 'I can't see Paul doing such a thing. There'd be no point. He's already wealthy in his own right, and there'd be no point in trying to sell what is basically his own brainchild. He's worked too hard on this project.'

'So who did Cindy see out on the lawn?' Lianne asked. 'The same person we saw?'

'Probably,' Ellen replied. 'She said he was stumbling, but she thought it was because he was in a hurry. Well he wasn't in a hurry when we saw him, but he still wasn't too good on those heels. So I reckon, whoever it was, that was the first time he'd ever worn that outfit, same as we worked out last night.'

'And we're left with the same suspects,' Lianne reminded her. 'But who else would stand to gain? James? Or Simon?'

'Well not Gavin,' Ellen decided. 'I mean, he might stand to gain, but it wasn't him inside the suit. He's too broad across the shoulders and it'd never fit him. He's also a fair bit taller than Paul and leather doesn't stretch too well.'

'So it had to be someone the same height and build as Paul?'

'Or a bit smaller. None of us could say for certain that the suit was a perfect fit,' Ellen mused. 'If it was a bit loose, who'd notice, either from a distance or in poor light?'

'That whittles it down to one then, doesn't it? Unless one of Nadia's guests fits the bill.'

Ellen shook her head. 'We know that one was a bit tied up at the critical times. He usually has a good long session when he's here – I know, because I've sneaked down to watch before now. And the other one, well if you see him you'll know what I mean. He's German – not that that's got anything to do with it – about six feet five and must weigh two hundred and eighty pounds – minimum. You'd need to slaughter a whole herd of cows to get enough leather to make a bodysuit for him!'

'Which brings us back to—'

'James,' Ellen finished for her quietly. 'Good old bad tempered James.'

'But they're his own drawings,' Lianne protested. 'Why would he steal his own work?'

'Who knows? I know he and Paul rarely see eye to eye over things,' Ellen said. 'James reckons Paul hasn't got his artistic gifts for imagining a scene as it would be best shown, and Paul has often had a go at James because he's taken liberties with the finished pictures. Maybe James fancies setting up on his own, or perhaps selling his wares to a higher bidder.'

'But, if that's the case, why is James still here and Paul gone?'

'Perhaps it's to divert suspicion?'

'But that would mean James has done something to Paul. Surely you don't think he would—'

'I don't know what to think,' Ellen cut Lianne short. 'But I'm pretty sure of two things. Firstly, James is our man and he's still here. Secondly, so are most of the pictures.'

'How on earth do you figure that one out?' Lianne demanded.

Ellen held up a hand and began counting off the fingers with the forefinger of the other. 'One, we saw the two of them by the gate. Two, the package that James – assuming it was him – passed over was far too small to hold more than perhaps the negatives. And three, with all the prints and drawings there would be too much stuff for one person to get out in one go.'

'Yeah, but hang on a minute,' Lianne interrupted. 'There were two of them, and we saw them going back for something or other. And we know that James was seen dragging a big case across the lawn.'

'I know all that,' Ellen agreed, 'but I've got another theory. Answer me this: why should James, or his sidekick in the van, bother kidnapping Paul, or whatever else they did with him?'

'I thought we'd already agreed that it was to throw suspicion on him.'

'Yes, but how about if that was just an afterthought?'

Lianne narrowed her eyes. 'Go on,' she said, 'I'm listening.'

Ellen began pacing back and forth across the room. 'Try this on for size,' she began. 'James decides to have the stuff away, but there are two problems. Firstly, the gear's bulky and you can't exactly hide it under your jacket. Secondly, there's only one way to get it to a vehicle, other than the main driveway, which is locked and in any case is covered by video cameras. The problem is, to get to the woods you have to cross a stretch of open ground and risk being seen from the house.

'The solution is to make people think it's someone else, so James gets hold of Paul's spooky suit and, sure enough, Cindy automatically assumes it's Paul she's seen, same as we did at first. Anyone else seeing him would think the same.' Ellen paused and pointed a finger straight at Lianne. 'Except for one person.'

'You mean Paul himself!' Lianne exclaimed, jumping up. 'So Paul decides to find out who's wearing his suit and follows into the woods?'

'But James realises he's been followed and gets the jump on him. That's why they were getting so excited down by the gate. James was explaining to the other guy that he's got a complication. And they can't risk leaving Paul here, so they both go back to carry him out between them. It'd be easier to hide the pictures than to conceal a man.'

'But what was to stop them going back for Paul and the pictures?' Lianne demanded. Ellen tapped the side of her nose with her forefinger.

'Elementary, my dear Watson. Time,' she said. 'Not that you'd be aware of it, but all the doors to the house are on a time lock and can only be opened from the inside between ten-thirty and seven the following morning. When we last saw them it would have already been close to ten, maybe even a few minutes after. By the time they collected Paul and lugged him back to the van, there would have been barely enough leeway for James to make it back before the locks went on. Don't forget, he was having trouble walking in those heels and it would have taken him longer than it took us.'

'So where did he hide the pictures?'

'That's the sixty-four thousand dollar question,' Ellen said. 'But I reckon we can narrow it down a bit. When we last saw them they weren't heading towards the house, so I reckon the barn was their destination. If James got the drop on Paul he'd only have knocked him out. He may be a worm, but he's not a murderer. Now I don't know about you, but I don't know how hard you've got to hit a man to make sure he stays out for more than a few minutes, and I doubt whether James does either.

'Depending upon where the fight took place, the nearest place to find something to immobilise Paul before he came round would have been the barn. There's a whole collection of restraint harnesses, chains and gags there. Now, just in case James doesn't make it back in

116

time, he decides against leaving the case with the pictures with Paul and so he drags it with him and hides it in the barn, returning to truss up Paul and maybe drag him to the barn afterwards as well.

'It'd take the two of them to shift Paul from the barn out to the gate, so the case has to be left behind for now. Later, when the rumpus dies down a bit, it's a simple matter to retrieve it and take it through the woods without all the disguise nonsense. The path from the barn to the perimeter can't be seen from the house.'

Lianne's eyes were wide with admiration. 'I think you've solved it,' she exclaimed. 'So let's go and tell Nadia.'

Ellen shook her head. 'Not yet. James would simply deny it. And even if we do find the case in the barn, it's no proof. Not only that, we still don't know where Paul is. No, I've got a better idea, but I need to think it out carefully first.'

CHAPTER THIRTEEN

At ten o'clock Suzy appeared to announce that the day's schedule had been suspended. Apparently the atmosphere was such that nobody was in the mood for work, and Nadia had announced that she was calling in a private detective agency to try to find the missing Paul, together, so she hoped, with the stolen pictures.

Ellen then did a disappearing act of her own for an hour, leaving Lianne to her own devices. When she returned she had a smug look on her face.

'You've found the stuff!' Lianne exclaimed. 'Why didn't you say you were going to look for it? You rotten cow!'

'I'm sorry,' Ellen said, though her voice lacked sincerity. 'I just thought it'd be better if just one of us went. It's less obvious.'

'So, where was it?'

'In the barn, same as we thought, though it took me a while to find it. He'd tucked it right into a corner with bales of straw and a load of old timber piled on top. By the way, I reckon we were right about Paul, too. I'm certain I saw a body-sack hanging up in the barn yesterday afternoon, but it's not there now.'

'What's a body-sack?' Lianne asked. Ellen explained that it was exactly what the name suggested; a leather cocoon that laced and strapped tightly around the victim, pinning their arms to their sides and their legs together.

'There's also a helmet attached with a built in gag. You get put in one of those, and there's no way you get out on your own.'

'And you reckon that's what they used on Paul?'

'Uh-huh, I'm sure of it. Unconscious or awake, it would have been useless for him to struggle. I just hope they don't keep him in it for too long,' Ellen added. 'I've tried it myself, and I can tell you it's dead uncomfortable.'

'So what do we do now?'

'We borrow one of Simon's cameras and we stake out the place tonight,' Ellen said. 'Or rather, I stake it out with the camera. I think Simon's got one of those night-sight telephoto lenses, so I can keep a distance between me and the barn. In the meantime you wait down by the gate, and when they're at the barn you sneak out and let down the tyres on the van.'

'What if the driver stays with the van?' Lianne asked.

'He won't,' Ellen replied confidently. 'The case Cindy saw James carrying was probably the second or third of three. At least, there's three hidden in the barn, so it'll need both of them to do the carrying. Those cases are full of paper stuff, and they're bloody heavy.'

'Well, I hope you know what you're doing,' Lianne said. 'I don't know why we don't just tell Nadia.'

'Because, my dear partner, the fewer people who know about this, the better. If James gets wind that anything's wrong he won't go within a mile of that barn, and that won't help Paul, now will it?'

'You sound as though you think I'm particularly worried about Paul.'

'And aren't you?'

'Well, of course I am, but no more than I would be if it were any of the rest of you,' Lianne protested.

Ellen gave her a wry smile. 'Naturally,' she said quietly.

CHAPTER FOURTEEN

Lianne was in position half an hour before dusk, crouching in the undergrowth about twenty yards from the gate, dressed from head to foot in black leather; a bodysuit and mask combination that hid everything but her eyes and mouth. Ellen was dressed similarly for her part in their joint mission, having pointed out that the less white flesh there was to reflect any moonlight, the better their chances would be of remaining undetected.

Darkness fell and it seemed that the elements were

on their side, for heavy cloud cover obscured the moon, so that someone could have passed within two feet of Lianne without realising she was there. However the van, if it was coming at all, was much later than the previous evening and, after another hour, Lianne was beginning to wish she had brought her cigarettes with her. She was just readjusting her cramped position when she detected the first distant sounds of an engine. The sound grew closer, and sure enough a few minutes later the van came into view, moving very slowly along the uneven track and stopping in the same place as before. Once again the driver waited for several minutes after switching off the ignition before he got out and made his way towards the gate.

He was not kept waiting for long, for another figure emerged from the woods carrying a heavy looking case, exactly as Ellen had described those she had discovered in the barn. His progress was much steadier than the night before, for this time he was not hampered by unfamiliar heels. James Naylor was wearing a dark shirt and jeans with a pair of black trainers, and this time there could be no doubts as to his identity.

As he reached the gate Lianne heard the two men exchanging greetings and James, depositing his burden for a few minutes, removed the padlock. The driver stepped through the open gate and the conversation continued for a few seconds more, before both men set off back along the path by which James had arrived. Lianne waited for what she judged was about a minute after they had disappeared from her view, and then began moving towards the open gate and the van which lay beyond.

The girls had earlier calculated that it would take James

and his companion five or six minutes to cover the distance to the barn, and possibly a minute longer for the return journey, weighed down as they would be by then. It was more than enough for Lianne's sabotage mission. The nail-file she clutched in her hand was the only tool she needed, and Ellen had explained how she should use it to depress the valve on each tyre. They had had no opportunity to rehearse beforehand, but Ellen had assured her that a minute would be plenty of time for each tyre.

'If you get problems with any of the tyres, move on to another,' she had said. 'You need to let down at least two, because they're bound to have a spare wheel. Three would be even better, just in case they're carrying a foot pump. By the time they manage to sort three wheels I'll have brought the cavalry from the house.'

The only thing Lianne had not been prepared for was the noise the escaping air made, for the violent hissing sounded more like a jet engine in the peaceful night atmosphere. Surely it would carry through the woods, but it was too late now; the job had to be completed. Grimly, she held the steel point hard into the valve and gritted her teeth, thankful to see the tyre rapidly losing its shape. This, she thought, was going to be easy. But that thought lasted less than three seconds, for as she made to straighten up, Lianne felt an arm coil itself around her throat and a hand grab the wrist that was holding the nail-file.

With a blinding flash of inspirational hindsight, Lianne saw the one flaw in Ellen's otherwise flawless plan – neither of them had considered the possibility that the van driver would not be alone! With a strength born of desperation Lianne almost managed to throw her assailant off, but he was very big and extremely powerful and, just when she thought she had eluded his grasp, he seized her around one ankle and threw her headlong into the undergrowth.

The impact of landing on the hard ground drove the breath from her lungs and sent her head spinning. She rolled over, trying to scramble to her feet again, but it was too late, for he pounced on her, knocking her flat on her back, and leapt astride her, pinning her with his superior weight and holding her wrists to the ground on either side of her head. Accepting the inevitable, Lianne went limp, gasping for air.

In the darkness it was impossible to see what the man looked like, though she sensed he was not all that old. His silhouette against the sky above suggested he had short hair and a broad face, but his features remained in shadow. Also, despite his efforts at subduing her, he did not seem to be even breathing heavily. Lianne saw the faint gleam of his eyes as they studied her.

'I don't know who you are,' she said, trying to keep the tremor of fear from her voice, 'but this is private property and you're trespassing.' Even as she said it, Lianne realised how pathetic that statement was, and it had about as much effect on the man as she had honestly expected. He let out a harsh laugh and leaned back a little, his weight pressing even more painfully on her abdomen.

'That motor is also private property,' he said, a sneer in his voice, 'and you were committing criminal damage.'

'I was not!' Lianne snapped. 'There's no damage to it at all – apart from a flat tyre – and you can easily pump that up again.'

'Maybe I should make you do it,' the man said. He

pulled her wrists together and held them both easily in one spade-like hand. With the other he began exploring Lianne's torso and head. 'Ah, so you're one of the tarts I've been hearing about,' he said. 'Pretty little leather lady in her kinky gear. Yeah, I've heard all about you lot.'

'From James Naylor, no doubt,' Lianne retorted. 'And you can keep your filthy hands to yourself!'

'Oh, is that so? Bit of a change of attitude that, from what I've been told. I thought you tarts just loved being helpless playthings. Well, maybe I'm not going about things the right way. I'll have to ask James when he gets back and I'm sure he'll be very curious to find you here.'

'Whatever he does, it won't do him any good,' Lianne snapped. 'By the time he gets here my friend will be back at the house, complete with photographs of him and your other friend bringing those cases out of the barn. His cover's blown, so you might as well chuck it in now.' The words were out before she had even thought about it and, the moment she did, Lianne could have bitten her tongue off. Now they would know that time was short and they wouldn't hang about arguing with her. She just hoped that Ellen's assessment of James Naylor proved to be an accurate one, and that he really was not a killer.

CHAPTER FIFTEEN

Nadia Muirhead slammed the receiver back onto its cradle in an uncharacteristic show of pique, and swore under her breath. Slowly, she looked around the assembled company, taking in the anxious faces, the worried eyes.

'They must have just missed them,' she said with undisguised frustration. 'Gavin parked the car right across the end of the bridge and waited, but they didn't appear, so they left Simon and Hazel in the car and he and Marcia walked along the track for about half a mile. He didn't want to risk the car on the bridge, but they went far enough on foot to a point where they could see the gate and there was no sign of the van.'

Ellen let out a groan of anguish. 'Damn! Still, at least we've got pictures of them. I just wonder why Lianne didn't do the tyres as we agreed. I hope nothing awful's happened to her.'

'Maybe she just lost her bottle at the last minute,' Suzy suggested, a scowl on her plump features. Ellen glared at her.

'She wouldn't do that!' she exclaimed. Cindy Fletcher, the fourth woman present, shook her head, her brow furrowed.

'If she didn't,' she said thoughtfully, 'then we must assume that they caught her.'

'But how could they? We had it all worked out. Lianne would have had a good ten minutes to do the job and get

124

clear.'

Nadia steepled her fingers together and leaned her elbows on the desk in front of her. 'I fear Cindy could be right,' she said. 'You see, I think you worked it all out very well, considering, but you may have overlooked one tiny point.'

'Such as what?' Ellen protested, her eyes wide with indignation. Nadia let out a long sigh and told her.

CHAPTER SIXTEEN

Lianne waited for several seconds after the door had closed, and then struggled into a sitting position, her back resting against the wall on the far side of the bed upon which she had been unceremoniously dumped. Her wrists were bound behind her back, and her ankles were still tied together with the rough rope that James Naylor had taken from the back of the van. She looked around the room, but what she saw was far from promising.

Apart from the narrow bed with its bare mattress, the only other item of furniture was a low stool. The floor was stone, and the single high window was protected on the outside by sturdy bars and on the inside by a steel mesh. The only illumination inside the small rectangular cell was from a single bulb, set in the ceiling and well out of reach.

'Shit!' she exclaimed, her voice echoing off the bare surfaces. 'Shit and double shit!' How could they have been so stupid not to have thought of there being a third man. And why hadn't she bothered looking first? If she crept up on the van quietly, she would surely have seen the man in the passenger seat. Okay, she wouldn't have been able to immobilise the vehicle, but at least she wouldn't now be a prisoner who didn't have the first idea as to the location of her prison.

Everything had happened quickly when James and his first accomplice had returned. Naturally, he had been astonished to see her, but he had recovered his composure quickly.

'We'll take her with us,' he announced, opening the back of the van and searching for the ropes. The driver had seemed less certain.

'Which one of them is she?' he wanted to know. James Naylor turned on him with a contemptuous snarl.

'How can I tell, under that mask?' he demanded. 'Judging from the size of her I'd say it's the new one – but it hardly matters, does it? We can't leave her here to blow the whistle on us.'

'There's another one in this with her,' the big man said, and quickly related what he knew about the photographs at the barn.

'Dammit!' For a few seconds it seemed as though this revelation might throw Naylor off balance, but he responded quickly. 'We'll take her anyway,' he decided. 'This has given me an idea. Things might be turning out for the better after all.'

The journey in the back of the van was uncomfortable, to say the least, with space being very restricted. Lianne lay curled up on the floor, jammed between two of the cases and the metal side of the vehicle, whilst Naylor sat on the third case, the flat wheel, having been quickly replaced with the spare, between himself and the rear doors. From her cramped position Lianne could not see out, and had no idea of the route they were taking as the van snaked along country roads at an alarming rate.

She tried reasoning with Naylor, pointing out that the penalties for kidnapping were severe, but his only response had been a threat to gag her with an oily rag if she didn't shut up. Ball gags were one thing, but a dirty rag was something else and discretion prevailed. Silence reigned for the remainder of the trip, which seemed interminable.

Lianne heard the crunching sound beneath the tyres as the van pulled off the surfaced road and onto gravel and, a few seconds later, she found herself being bundled out into the night air. It was almost as dark there as it had been by the gate at the estate, but she had a brief impression of an old and isolated house before some sort of sacking was thrown over her head and she was hoisted up and draped over someone's shoulder. From the ease with which he handled her, Lianne guessed it was the man from the passenger seat who had originally captured her.

Again, with only her ears to provide her with any information, Lianne guessed that they had entered the house, for the sound of crunching gravel beneath the man's boots gave way to a much softer sound, suggesting carpet. That, in turn, gave way to what sounded like stone and then, after a brief pause and the sound of bolts being drawn back, a door creaked open and Lianne was thrown onto something that was at least partially soft. The sacking was dragged off, and without a word the big man spun on his heel and was gone. The dull thud of the bolts being replaced sounded, to Lianne, like nails being hammered into her coffin.

Her initial fears slowly subsiding, Lianne began to think, trying to respond as she was sure Ellen would have done had their positions been reversed. Okay, so she had been caught, abducted, and was in a pretty invidious, not to say uncomfortable, position. Presumably Paul Dean was also somewhere in the building and, also presumably, in a similar situation to her own. Also in the building were the stolen drawings and photographs. So far, so bad – score three points to the Naylor creep.

On the other hand Ellen was still free, always assuming – Lianne shuddered at the prospect – that she wasn't lying in a pool of blood somewhere near the barn.

'Don't be a morbid cow,' she said aloud. 'Whatever these creeps are, same as Ellen said, they're not murderers, otherwise you'd be dead yourself.'

Conclusion?

Ellen *was* alive, so Ellen had by now raised the alarm. Lianne closed her eyes, thinking hard. Of course Ellen was still alive! The big guy had told Naylor about her and that was the first he had known about it. A wave of relief flooded over Lianne and her eyes began to fill with tears. She shook her head to clear them – angry with herself; doing the emotional female bit wouldn't help anyone at this juncture, she lectured herself fiercely.

So, Ellen was alive, the alarm had been raised, and… And what? Lianne didn't even know where she was, so how could the rest of them? She was pretty certain that Nadia would not call in the authorities just yet. If the police got involved she would be risking everything she had. So what was the alternative?

Of course! For the second time in as many minutes Lianne hit upon an answer that swept away her worst doubts and fears. Nadia had money – lots of money.

And people with lots of money had lots of clout, lots of friends, and lots of contacts. Yes, Nadia might not want the police involved, but there were plenty of private concerns available for hire and, from what Lianne had read, they were often more effective than the official boys in blue; not having to tread carefully around so many niceties. Ergo, sit tight and wait and everything would come right in the end.

If only, Lianne thought, she didn't feel so bloody uncomfortable and so damned hungry!

CHAPTER SEVENTEEN

Only a matter of a few yards from where Lianne was languishing, although neither of them was aware of it, Paul Dean was also feeling bloody uncomfortable and damned hungry. He was also feeling very angry, very foolish, and very sorry for himself.

His anger was largely directed at James Naylor, for although he had never quite seen eye to eye with the man, they had been part of the same successful team and what Naylor had done was nothing more nor less than an act of betrayal. However, Paul had reserved a fair proportion of that anger to direct against himself, feeling foolish because he had allowed himself to be ambushed so easily. The self-pity was largely a result of the throbbing lump behind his left ear, a painful reminder of the moment when his world had exploded in a dazzling firework display of exploding lights.

Quite what this was all about Paul could not yet be

sure, but he had a shrewd idea. That case had been heavy, judging by the effort Naylor had expended in carrying it and, unless it was full of bricks or lead weights, there was only one other thing – leaving aside gold bars for the obvious reason – that Paul knew could weigh so much per cubic foot.

Paper.

Paper in all its various guises, including photographic paper. The bastard had been making off with the results of all their combined efforts! Quite why, Paul was not yet sure, but he just knew his basic premise was right. It had to be that, otherwise why all the subterfuge and why use his, Paul's, padded bodysuit to disguise his identity?

Naylor must have had a better offer, Paul concluded, for it was the only possible scenario. The man was also full of his own importance and thought everyone else on the team was his inferior in every way. Yes, that was it – someone else was willing to stake him in his own operation and, rather than start again from scratch, Naylor had decided upon a short cut. Paul swore to himself and tried, for at least the twentieth time, to see if there was any way he could work his wrists free of the steel manacles that shackled them behind his back. There wasn't.

With a sigh of frustration he turned onto his opposite side, trying to ease the cramps that were threatening his squashed left arm.

When the door finally reopened and James Naylor strode in, Lianne felt surprisingly calm. She stared out at him through the eye apertures in her mask, her chin at a defiant angle.

'You're in dead trouble,' she said, but the words were scarcely out of her mouth before his arm swung in a wide arc, his open hand smashing into her leather covered cheek. Yellow, red and purple lights exploded before her eyes and she fell back, gasping in pain.

'Where are they?' Naylor's question scythed through the coloured fog, but Lianne was as perplexed as she was hurt. Shaking her head and blinking away the tears of pain, she stared up at him.

'What?' she stammered, trying to draw herself into a defensive ball. 'What are you talking about?' Naylor's face was a mask of apoplectic rage. He leaned over her, his right hand curled into a fist.

'Don't mess with me!' he rasped. 'You know exactly what I'm talking about. Where are they – the pictures? The drawings? The photographs?'

'What pictures?' Lianne shouted back, panic and pain sending her voice soaring an octave. 'You've got the only pictures I know about!'

Naylor drew back his arm and Lianne screwed her eyes tightly shut, tensing herself for the blow, but it never came. Instead she felt Naylor's hand close around her lower jaw, his fingers gripping painfully through the leather. She opened her eyes again and stared up at him. His face was red with undisguised rage.

'Don't get cute with me, you deviant little whore,' he snarled. 'There was nothing in those cases except a load of stones and old lengths of chain, plus a few bin-bags full of rotten kitchen waste. So where's the stuff I put in them?'

Lianne continued to stare up at him, totally uncomprehending for several seconds. And then the penny dropped.

Despite her dire predicament she began to laugh hysterically, giggling and coughing, almost choking on her hysteria. Her reaction seemed to completely phase Naylor, for he released his grip on her and stepped back, his facial expression betraying his total uncertainty. At last Lianne managed to get a grip on herself.

'She's had you, hasn't she?' she almost screamed. 'Ellen, I mean. The cunning bitch never said a word to me, but she's dealt you a complete lemon. That's where she disappeared to this morning. She was filling your cases with rubbish, just in case. Oh my, that's *so* funny. Yeah, go ahead and beat me, you big brave wanker. It won't do you any good. You've gone to all this trouble for nothing. Nadia's still got everything and there's no way you'll get your thieving hands on it now.'

She tensed herself, waiting for the inevitable assault, watching Naylor's complexion run through the rainbow gamut, but the expected beating did not materialise. Slowly, James Naylor regained control of his temper, though his eyes were cold and frightening, nonetheless. He leaned over Lianne, one hand brushing lightly across her left cheek.

'For a tart you've got a high opinion of yourself,' he said menacingly. 'But there's an old saying about there being more than one way to skin a cat – perhaps you've heard of it? Well, little tart, you were all set to be the star of Nadia bloody Muirhead's new epic, so I reckon you'll do for me.' Lianne continued to stare up at him.

'What are you talking about?' she eventually said, her voice barely more than a whisper.

Naylor grinned at her, his mouth twisting cruelly. 'Simple, my little leather princess,' he said. 'We'll just have to start from scratch. I'd always intended to set up my own operation anyway. Taking back the existing pictures was just a short cut to getting started. Over the next few weeks I was going to finish my recruiting programme. I already have the nucleus of a new team, but I was having trouble finding two new heroines. Well,' he continued, 'it seems to me I now have them.'

'If you mean me,' Lianne retorted, picking up his train of thought immediately, 'you can forget it.'

Naylor straightened up, grinning smugly. 'I think not,' he said. 'There's a little something I've been working on for months that I think might convince you. By this time tomorrow you'll be begging me to let you cooperate.'

Lianne tried to ignore the icy fist that was clawing at her stomach. She shook her head defiantly.

'Okay, brave man that you are,' she said, her voice neutral. 'So you can do what you want with me, or so you think. But who's the other so-called heroine?' Naylor chuckled and shook his head in turn.

'None other than your own very favourite girl-with-a-cock,' he leered. 'Someone we already know brings out the very best animal instincts in you.'

'You're talking in riddles,' Lianne said. 'You should take more water with it.' For a second or two Lianne thought she had gone too far, for Naylor's features darkened and contorted into a mask of pure hatred. However, at the last moment, he managed to control himself once more.

'You won't be so bloody insolent when you see what I've got in mind,' he said. 'Mr Dean loves playing the girl-with-a-cock bit, so I reckon we should give full rein to his undoubted talents. It'll make a nice twist, as it happens. And by the time I'm through with you, you'll both be more than willing to go along with anything I want. After that, I think I might even have you myself. There's something about those big stupid eyes of yours that's almost appealing!'

Paul Dean stared up at James Naylor in derisive disbelief.

'You're out of your tiny box if you think I'm going to cooperate with you, Jimmy,' he snarled. 'Why don't you just let me and the girl go and cut your losses? It was a crazy scheme in the first place.'

Naylor shook his head, his expression betraying nothing. 'The scheme was sound enough,' he replied. 'It was just unlucky for me in the first place that you spotted me wearing that damned silly female suit thing of yours, and even unluckier that those two interfering females happened to be in the wrong place at the wrong time. That Ellen is a smarter cow than I'd have given her credit for, though luckily she made one small mistake, or we might have been in trouble.'

'You still didn't get the stuff,' Paul pointed out.

'No, but we've got you and the other girl and that could be even better in the long run.' Naylor smiled his peculiarly lopsided smile. 'You see, Paulie, we've been well behind the times in what we've been doing up until now. The strip cartoon idea was pretty novel, I must admit, but technology is marching ahead by the day. I'm bringing in a few fresh faces, and the most important is this software guy I've been talking to for the past few weeks.

'You won't believe what he can do with computer graphics,' he continued. 'Did you know, from a basic set of drawings he can produce a fully animated cartoon adventure. When I say a basic set, of course, it's a bit more than just a few sketches, but he can cut the number of hand originated frames required for an hour's worth of animated action by ninety-eight percent.'

'So you're going into the movie business,' Paul sneered. 'Walt Disney would turn in his grave.'

Naylor leaned over Paul's prone form. 'Not just the movies, Paulie,' he said. 'You and the amateur detective in there are gonna be big stars on the Internet. That's where tomorrow's big money is, believe me.'

'Well you'll have to get yourself another writer,' Paul said defiantly.

Again the crooked smile. 'Writer?' Naylor said, affecting surprise. 'Who said anything about needing a writer? I reckon I can produce scripts as good as yours, if not better. No Paulie, you're gonna be a star in person. You're gonna be an *actor*! You and sweet little Lianne are gonna make a great team. She can carry on in much the same sort of role Nadia signed her for, and you can replace the hardly inimitable Miss Sanderson.'

'It won't work nearly as well,' Paul said, despite himself. 'You know it was the two-damsels-in-distress scenario that sold the stories.'

'Quite so,' Naylor agreed. 'But your antics with that damned suit of yours have given me a few ideas. When I said that you could replace Ellen, I meant that literally. I reckon you'd make a pretty good female in bondage and I can make up for any slight differences with a few pen strokes here and there.'

'Why bother?' Paul said. 'Why not just get yourself another female actress?'

'Oh, I have my reasons,' Naylor said, turning towards the door. 'For a start, I don't have to pay you, or Lianne.

135

Secondly, bringing in outsiders would be a security risk. Lianne starts spouting off and we have a problem. The rest of my new cast, the ones playing the bad guys, are all sound. They're so far into the dominance thing that they'd probably play their parts for nothing, if I asked them.

'And thirdly,' he said, his hand resting on the door handle, 'I owe you a few. I never got the credit I was entitled to, not with you snivelling around that bitch Nadia's crotch all day long. Now I'm the one in charge, and I'm quite looking forward to seeing the high and mighty Paul Dean in a skirt.'

'You've lost the plot completely, Jimmy!' Paul exploded. 'You're barking! If you really think I'm going to—'

'You'll do whatever I say,' Naylor cut across his protestations. 'I'll be back later to show you something which I can guarantee will change your mind – and you can stick your mortgage on that, I promise!'

CHAPTER EIGHTEEN

Two of them came for Lianne just when she was beginning to think she had been completely forgotten. She recognised the passenger from the van, the man who had caught her, from his sheer size. Standing over six feet, he had to weigh at least seventeen stone and very little of that was fat. Now she could see his features properly, Lianne had to admit he was not at all bad looking in a rough sort of way.

His companion was much shorter and lighter built. He too had close cut hair, though of a much darker brown and his features were narrow and angular, suggestive of a short temper. Lianne guessed he was probably the van driver, but she could not be sure.

They removed the rope from her ankles but left her wrists tied behind her back as they escorted her down an uneven passage and out into a paved yard. Looking up, Lianne saw it was just beginning to get light, but the shadows between the house and the barn-like building towards which they guided her were deep and unrevealing.

Inside the barn, however, it was as bright as a midsummer's day. Huge overhead arc lamps illuminated everything, from the small swimming pool to the heavy trestled frame, the ominous looking post with its dangling straps and chains, and the semi-circle of armchairs which had been arranged facing the water. There were also several large crates scattered about the floor area, two of which had been prised open.

James Naylor rose from one of the armchairs as they entered. Behind him three other figures, all female, also rose. Lianne stared in disbelief, for the first of the trio was the tallest woman she had ever seen. Naylor clicked his fingers and the Amazon stepped forward. She would have dwarfed him even without the heels of the long white boots she was wearing. She also had incredibly well developed shoulders and arms, probably the result of a lifetime spent working out, but unlike most female bodybuilders she was far from flat-chested. In fact, the white leather leotard was struggling to contain a pair of breasts that Lianne guessed were double D at the minimum; their size emphasised by the woman's tiny waist and broad hips. Her face, though broad-featured, was undoubtedly very beautiful and the close shaven white blonde hair, which could have looked gauche on many women, merely added to her undeniable appeal.

The two women behind her were also pretty impressive and only the presence of the amazon detracted from their personal physical preferences. They were both dressed identically to the blonde, except in their cases the leather was black. The first one was Asian, with long straight jet-black hair and huge almond eyes. The second was dark-haired too, though it was brown rather than black and formed a curly halo about her head.

Lianne's escorts halted her about a pace from the blonde giantess and Naylor stepped forward, his smile wide and his eyes gleaming.

'I'd like to introduce Christina,' he said, indicating the blonde. 'She's from Denmark and she is your new mistress.'

Lianne let out a derisive snort. 'Oh, I get it,' she sneered. 'Stereotypical Scandinavian dominatrix scenario; hardly very original.' She regretted the taunt almost as soon as she had thrown it, for Christina stepped forward and dealt her an open-handed slap across her left cheek. Lianne's head exploded in a fountain of coloured lights and her ears rang for several seconds. If the two men had not been supporting her she would have fallen. Through the roar of pain, Lianne heard the Dane speak.

'I will tolerate none of your insolence,' she said in perfect English, with only the faintest trace of an accent. 'And that was only a gentle warning. Here we are not playing at the silly games – we are doing it for real. You do not get to go home after your day's work, either. You may not even get to sleep, for if I decide so, you will do a night's work as well.

'You will address me as Mistress when permitted to speak, and you will address my two assistants as Miss. This is Miss Marika and this is Miss Jodie.' As Lianne's vision cleared, she saw the woman indicate the Asian girl first and the curly brunette second. 'We should be absolutely clear from the start,' she continued. 'I do not enjoy making my slaves suffer... I positively *revel* in it. However, I am not an unjust mistress and good behaviour is always rewarded.

'I appreciate total obedience in a slave and will not tolerate rebellion or insubordination. I am also an expert in devising forms of punishment that are as painful as they are humiliating, so you would be well advised to heed my words. Now, get down on your knees, slavegirl.'

The downward pressure from the two men was scarcely required as Lianne hastened to obey. If that slap was a "gentle warning", she was in no rush to find out what the Dane could do if she got serious. The woman stepped closer and seized Lianne's head between her powerful hands.

'Leather!' she snorted. 'The only leather I permit on a slave is as a harness or a restraint. My slaves wear rubber – if they wear anything at all.' She turned her head and looked over her shoulder at her two assistants. 'Strip our little captive,' she ordered.

It did not take them very long to carry out the order, for it was obvious that the two women were experts at their job. Lianne was lifted to her feet again, and the leather bodysuit and hood were unbuckled, unlaced and peeled away, leaving her standing naked. In her bare feet and without her heels Lianne felt even smaller and more vulnerable standing before the imposing trio of women.

Christina bent forward and stroked Lianne's denuded vulva appreciatively.

'Very nice,' she said. 'A slave should always be hairless. Later perhaps, we shall shave your head too; there is a certain appeal about that.' She placed a hand beneath each of Lianne's breasts and hefted them as if she were weighing them against each other. The sheer impersonal nature of the examination made Lianne shiver, but she knew her nipples were already reacting to the touch of flesh upon flesh. The fact was not lost on Christina either. She transferred her attention to the pouting peaks, tweaking them between thumb and forefinger.

'These will have to be pierced and ringed,' she announced, though to nobody in particular. 'In fact, I shall do it now. It will save time after we have completed the slave's initiation.' Lianne felt her stomach lurch at the words. Her immediate impulse was to cry out in protest, but she managed to stifle her reaction, realising that not only would it do absolutely no good, but that any show of rebellion or dissent would bring spiteful retribution as swift as it would be painful.

The Asian girl, Marika, strode across to one of the open cases and began rummaging in it. After only a few seconds she found what she was looking for; a metal box about twelve inches by eight and about three inches deep. She carried it back to Christina, opened the lid, and presented it to her. Lianne was just able to catch a glimpse of what was inside the box and she shut her eyes, trembling in trepidation.

It was actually a lot less awful than she had anticipated, though the shock of the freezing spray when it hit her nipples made her jump and squeal in surprise. Whatever was in the aerosol worked rapidly and thoroughly, for when Christina pushed the wicked looking needle through Lianne's puckered flesh, she felt nothing at all. The rings were thick and about an inch and a half in diameter, formed in two halves that swivelled away from each other to enable them to be threaded through the fresh holes. When they were in place Christina simply swivelled them back into line and pressed the thinner prong of one end into the hollow end of the other. The two ends met with a decisive click and, staring down at the first ring whilst Christina fitted the second, Lianne could not see how they were supposed to be removed again.

It was as though the Dane could read her thoughts.

'In case you were wondering, slave,' she said, snapping home the second ring, 'the only way these can be removed is if they are cut off. They are gold plated, but their cores are stainless steel, for added strength. So, as far as you are concerned, these rings are now permanent.' She turned to Marika, who was closing the lid of the box. 'You know what I want now, don't you?' she said. The Asian girl nodded, her huge eyes sparkling as she turned away towards the open case once more. Christina looked down at Lianne, and her mouth twitched in what might just have been the beginning of a smile.

'I am now going to restrain you, temporarily, whilst we fit the first part of your costume,' she said. 'This particular form of restraint I devised myself and it is particularly effective in preventing recalcitrant slaves from struggling. Be thankful that you will only be wearing it for a few minutes today. Later, you may not be so lucky.'

Lianne looked past her to where James Naylor was lounging back in his armchair, clearly enjoying the proceedings. She wished she could smash her fist into his smug face, for he was obviously enjoying her plight. He saw her watching him and taunted her with a wave.

'Oh, I forgot to tell you,' he called across to her, 'that all of this is being recorded on video. I have a much more advanced set-up here. If you look up into the rafters you can just make out the cameras. There are six of them in all and they are all computer controlled, with zoom lenses and everything. The results really do have to be seen to be believed.'

Christina's invention was as simple as it was devilish and consisted of two steel wrist cuffs, each attached to a length of chain. The cuffs were locked into place and Lianne's arms pulled behind her back and lifted until her forearms were parallel with the floor. The chain from her right wrist was then passed up her back and over her left shoulder, drawn diagonally across her chest and attached to the ring on her right nipple by means of a spring clip. The reverse process was then carried out on her other wrist and nipple. Now the slightest downward pressure from her arms would tug each breast upwards, stretching it out of shape and distorting the nipples painfully.

'Of course,' Christina said, 'the anaesthetic hasn't yet worn off, so you won't feel the full effect today – but it should still suffice. Right girls, start getting her ready.'

They forced Lianne to lay down on her back – an uncomfortable position with her arms trapped behind her, but she had little choice other than to obey. From another chest the brunette called Jodie pulled out what Lianne guessed was a rubber bodysuit. Her guess proved correct, but it was a bodysuit unlike any she had seen before.

It was made from heavy latex and was already powdered. Though the two assistants had to struggle to get Lianne's feet into the sealed bottoms and the rubber felt tight, outwardly it looked to be loose and floppy. It took them a couple of minutes to pull the leggings up and around her hips, for the back zipped opening extended only down as far as the tops of her buttocks.

Satisfied that her prisoner was properly sheathed from the waist down, Christina produced a flat board, made from two hinged sections with holes for the ankles. Once it was locked in place Lianne was forced to sit with her legs stretched apart almost as far as they would go. The position was neither comfortable nor dignified, but at least the chains were removed from her wrists and nipples to enable them to fit the remainder of the suit.

Once again, as with her feet, it was a struggle to get her fingers into the gloves on the end of the sleeves and yet, outwardly, her hands did not seem to be gloved at all, for all that was visible was a loose and floppy mitten. But Lianne had little chance to consider this as Jodie then took a brush and drew her hair up into an even higher ponytail, before the final stage of drawing the fitted hood over Lianne's head was completed.

As it was tugged down into place and sealed to the collar, two blue tinted lenses came into position over Lianne's eyes and a strange sort of mouthpiece affair aligned with her lips, pressing against her mouth awkwardly. Lianne assumed it was some sort of gag, which in a way it was, but when it was pushed between her lips she realised it was designed to hold her mouth open, rather than to fill it; there being a stiff circular aperture in its centre. However, in its own fashion, it was as effective at preventing coherent speech as the earlier ball gags had been, but the reason for the opening became very clear the moment Lianne tried to breathe in through her nose. Her best efforts met with nothing, and she realised that the mask had no holes for her nostrils at all, the molded rubber simply sealing off her nose completely. Alarm bells started ringing in the back of her head, but there was absolutely nothing she could do.

The mystery of the loose rubber at the ends of her arms and about her feet was now revealed. Marika produced a small compressed air cylinder from the crate. There was a short length of hose attached to its nozzle and a connector valve fitted to the free end. This valve was swiftly attached to a corresponding valve at the end of each limb in turn and the loose rubber was inflated to produce four perfectly rounded balls. Lianne stared at each of them, totally perplexed.

Heavy rubber straps were then buckled around her ankles and wrists and the board removed from around the former. The lower straps were connected to each other by a length of chain and the wrists similarly connected to a rubber belt which Marika buckled around Lianne's waist, though the chain lengths were sufficiently slack for her to very nearly extend her arms to the horizontal.

Meanwhile, Jodie had been busy removing her leather boots and unzipping her leather leotard, shrugging it off to reveal a brief pair of rubber panties underneath.

Naked apart from these, she carefully drew a black rubber swim cap over her curls, tucking away loose strands of hair until none was left showing. She moved smoothly to the edge of the pool and dived with lithe finesse into the water. At a nod from Christina, Marika and the two men, who had been standing well back throughout the preparations, joined her in grasping one of Lianne's limbs apiece and lifting her into the air.

Seeing what was intended she at last began to struggle, but she was no match for the four of them. They passed her arms down to Jodie who was calmly treading water, and a moment later Lianne found herself floating on her back, her hands and feet bobbing on the surface, buoyed by the inflated balls. She was dimly aware of Jodie flipping headfirst beneath the water, her feet describing a graceful arc as she dived. A few seconds later Lianne felt a tug at the back of her waist belt, but she could not turn her head to see what was happening beneath her.

Jodie surfaced blowing air, and now Lianne saw the long hose that Marika passed down to her. There was a sort of threaded attachment at one end and, whilst Lianne stared along the length of her rubber covered nose in horror, Jodie began screwing it into the mouth aperture in the mask.

'The other end fits to a float,' she explained to the helpless Lianne as she tightened the connection, 'so you'll get plenty of air down there.' Marika was already taking care of that problem, clipping the free end of the tube through the middle of a cork rectangle and dropping it into the pool alongside the two girls.

Jodie made one final check on the mask and gave the thumbs up sign to the poolside watchers. Lianne saw with horror that Christina was holding one end of a chain that disappeared into the pool just where they had lowered her in. As she watched helplessly, the striking Dane began to pull steadily on that chain.

Immediately Lianne felt the tug at her back again and began drifting out into the middle of the pool as the slack was taken up. She was soon over the point where the chain ran through whatever anchorage was on the bottom, for now she began to descend, her bottom going first, her buoyed hands and feet remaining above the surface until just after her head had dipped beneath the water. She continued to descend for a few more feet before coming to a halt, but there was little cause for relief.

Her position was almost impossible; hands floating upwards as far as the chains would allow, her feet up level with her face, and her body bent almost double at the waist. Sucking wildly at the mouthpiece, Lianne was barely aware as the suntanned shape dived past her, but she did see the hand grabbing at her ankle chain and was mightily relieved when her legs were dragged downwards to something nearer the vertical position. As her head came forward again in response to her body's shift of plane, Lianne saw that Jodie was clipping her hobble to the chain which had pulled her under, so that now she was held in a position not unlike that of a long jumper in mid-jump.

She strained to look upwards, in total bewilderment, as Jodie flashed past her again. She watched the woman's lower body as she broke the surface and paddled her way gently towards the poolside. Buttocks, legs, and then feet disappeared through the mirrored underside of the surface as Jodie climbed out... and then Lianne was left alone. She was left bobbing helplessly in her own watery world, the silence broken only by the sound of her heart thumping and the air rasping in and out of her throat.

Paul Dean stared down at the black figure beneath the water, horrified yet fascinated by the ingenuity of Lianne's aquatic bondage. Beside him James Naylor wore a superior look on his face.

'She's only been down there for half an hour,' he said, 'but I'm told it'll seem like five times that to her. This idea is based on the isolation tanks they use for sensory deprivation experiments. Even the water is kept at body temperature. She isn't blindfolded, as you can probably see, but the surface tension of the water and the refractive index means that she can't see out. She'll be feeling pretty lonely by now, I should think.'

'You're a real bastard, Jimmy,' Paul snarled. His arms were cuffed behind his back, but he had to fight back the urge to drive his forehead into the artist's superior smirk and then kick him into the pool. It would give him a little short-lived satisfaction, but he knew there were too many of them to fight, and it would do Lianne no good whatsoever.

Naylor turned away nonchalantly, hands in pockets. 'You can get her out of there, Paulie,' he said. 'You only have to say the word.'

'Never – I'll not humiliate myself like that!' Paul shouted. Naylor shrugged.

'I don't see what the big deal is. After all, you've dressed up as a woman before now. I've seen you pull that stunt with the suit at least half a dozen times.'

'That's totally different.'

Naylor turned back to face Paul. 'I know it is, pal,' he

sneered. 'Which is what makes it so precious. Macho Paul Dean in a skirt and stockings, taking the role of a female slave even more arduous than the ones he's so fond of creating.'

'You're completely twisted!'

'The words pot and kettle spring to mind,' Naylor taunted. 'But it's up to you. We can always drug you and get you dressed suitably whilst you're out for the count, but then the little mermaid stays down there for a further twenty-four hours. I should imagine she'd be even more barking than you seem to think I am by the time we let her up. And I'm willing to bet she'd do anything – and I do mean anything – rather than go back down there again.'

Paul's shoulders sagged, for the mad gleam in James Naylor's eyes was evidence enough that the man was totally capable of carrying out his threats. He could let them drug him and then refuse to cooperate afterwards, but the thought of letting Lianne stay in the pool for so long, plus the fact that they would only return her to the pool if he did give them trouble, outweighed everything else. He shrugged, trying not to betray the desperation that was threatening to overwhelm his soul.

'Okay,' he said, 'you win – for now. But there's always tomorrow.'

Naylor nodded and smiled. 'There is,' he agreed. 'And the day after tomorrow, and the day after that, and the day after that. There's always tomorrow, Paulie, but all yours, for the foreseeable future, are going to be spent as a pretty female slave, co-starring with the water baby down there.'

CHAPTER NINETEEN

Lianne could not believe it when they told her she had been underwater for less than an hour, for it had seemed like an eternity and she was completely disoriented when they finally dragged her up to the surface. Strangely though, she had not been scared, at least not after the first few minutes. Floating there in limbo she had experienced a detached tranquility she had never known before; a feeling of safe isolation from anything the world could offer as a threat. Nevertheless, she was still relieved to be back on dry land.

Christina stood over Lianne as her two assistants went about the task of removing the rubber suit. She looked down at the panting girl with a strange expression on her face, and then knelt beside her and stroked her forehead with surprising tenderness.

'You and I were destined for each other,' she said quietly. 'You were made for me as no other before has been, and it is a sin that you should be wasted on so many unappreciative philistines. But never fear, my little angel, for Christina will take care of your needs before it is done.'

James Naylor was less gentle. 'Well,' he exclaimed, prodding her buttocks with the toe of his boot, 'how does it feel to experience the real thing? It certainly had the desired effect on darling Paul. It nearly cracked him up, seeing you down there. And if he doesn't act like a good girlie, back you go.'

Lianne was puzzled by his choice of words, but she remained silent, hardly caring what they did to her now. It was as though she were watching events from somewhere above herself now, and although it was her body they were handling, she no longer felt that she were a part of it. She smiled up at Naylor and sighed.

'Where is he?' she said. 'I want him.'

Naylor let out a harsh laugh. 'You'll have him soon enough, girlie,' he sneered. 'They're making him presentable as we speak, but first we have to see to you. Christina has a few ideas of her own, so I've told her to go ahead. It should prove very interesting.'

Lianne's costume certainly did prove interesting, and Christina and Jodie spent quite a while getting her into it, for it was far more severe than anything she had been asked to wear back at the estate.

The main item was a sleeveless rubber leotard, with a high neckline and cutouts for her breasts and her buttocks. The latter were bad enough; squeezing her nates into two prominent mounds, but the former were even worse, the holes being so small that they forced her breasts out into two prominent melon shapes, stretching her skin and making her pierced nipples jut out like two hat pegs. There was also an oval aperture that left her denuded sex exposed. The garment zipped at the back, but there were also three straps that were then tightened to constrict Lianne's waist like a corset. When they finally finished adjusting it she felt as though she were being squeezed in a vice.

Long rubber gloves were then drawn up her arms, but over these went a leather sleeve, drawing her upper limbs together behind her back and forcing her distended breasts out even further. It was a far from comfortable posture, but Lianne, looking down at herself, found that all she could think of was the prospect of someone's mouth sucking on her ringed teats! The thought started a fierce fire in her loins and it was all she could do to prevent herself from crying out.

The long rubber boots were not that dissimilar from what she had worn before, except that the heels were ridiculously high and only her toes actually touched the floor. Dimly, as she tried to control the fires that were now burning within her, she registered the fact that she would have trouble standing in them – let alone walking.

Walking, however, did not appear to be on the agenda, for no sooner had they finished lacing the boots than a second leather tube, similar to the one that encased her arms only longer and larger, was wrapped about her legs and the lacing process started all over. When it was finished her two legs were as one, pressed together in an unyielding embrace.

'It seems a shame to cover such a pretty face,' Christina said, 'but it is necessary to do these things correctly.' She snapped her fingers at Jodie, who as if by magic, produced the rubber helmet. 'We must fill this sweet mouth to still its noise,' Christina whispered as she pulled the hood over Lianne's head. 'But fear not, my beautiful slave, for I will find a better use for those luscious lips before this day is finished.'

Paul Dean looked from Marika to the huge form of Eric Raines, who was leaning casually against the door, tapping a leather-covered baton against the palm of his hand. Paul had already looked around the room in search of something – anything – that he could use as a weapon once his hands were free, but there was nothing obvious and he saw that even the padded stool was bolted into the stone floor.

Marika, it appeared, was still not prepared to take any chances and it was obvious that she was an expert in her chosen vocation. She manoeuvreed Paul into the centre of the room, beneath the slim chain that dangled from the opening in the ceiling, and moved behind him to clip the end of it onto the link that joined his wrist cuffs. She moved over to the wall, flipped back a cover to reveal a set of switches, and flicked one. Immediately from above came the sound of an electric motor and Paul found his wrists being drawn inexorably upwards, pulling his arms away from his back and forcing him to bend at the waist. Just as he thought she intended to suspend him from his arms, probably dislocating his shoulders in the process, Marika flicked the switch again and the motor stopped.

'That should keep you out of trouble for the time being,' she said as she walked back across to him. He had never before felt so vulnerable; trussed there naked and helpless before a woman whose every syllable seemed to drip contempt, and she emphasised their respective positions by idly taking hold of his flaccid penis and waggling it to and fro. 'We'll have to see what can be done about waking this up later,' she laughed, releasing her grip and moving across to the old fashioned chest of drawers in the corner. 'Meantime, let's see what we can do about prettying you up.'

Lianne was not having a particularly comfortable time, for when it became apparent that Marika's preparations with the other slave were taking longer than expected, Christina decided to amuse herself with her new plaything. Lifting Lianne effortlessly in her arms she carried her across to one of the trestle frames, stood her in front of it, and bent her forward over the horizontal bar.

Quickly she locked a wide collar about Lianne's throat, attaching a chain to one of the steel rings set into it, and drew the free end down, winding it about her ankles and securing it with a padlock to prevent the helpless girl from straightening up again.

'I think a quick spanking, just to get you warmed up,' the sensuous Dane drooled. She went to one of the crates and drew out a pair of white leather gauntlets. Even from her doubled over position Lianne saw that the insides of the fingers had been reinforced with thick rubber strips. The surfaces of the strips had been roughened, as she discovered when Christina began to stroke the compressed flesh of her buttocks, which protruded through the cutouts in the leotard.

'Canes and whips cause more pain,' Christina whispered, bending close to Lianne's ear, 'but a spanking is so much more personal, I always think. With the bare hand is even more intimate, but I wish to try out my new spanking gloves and this is the ideal opportunity.' She continued her abrasive caresses for several more seconds before putting the gloves to the test. When she did, the sharp crack as the rubber slapped into Lianne's unprotected flesh echoed throughout the cavernous barn, almost as loudly as Lianne's screech of shock and pain.

Abruptly, Christina stepped back and motioned to Jodie. 'I was forgetting,' she said, 'that this one is still a novice. Gag her please – fully.'

It was almost a relief when the rubber ball was slipped between Lianne's teeth, even though the external pad that clamped over her lips when the strap was tightened was very uncomfortable. Lianne bit into the comforting rubber and, although she tried to yell when the second slap landed, the gag was so effective that hardly a sound escaped.

'Much better,' Christina commented calmly, and proceeded to spank Lianne steadily and severely. Lianne grunted and groaned, tears filling her eyes, but there was nothing she could do except take the unjust punishment. She screwed her eyes shut and prayed that the woman would stop... but then, just as she was beginning to think she could take no more, the burning sensations began to change. Her buttocks still bucked and reared with every blow, but the fire of pain was slowly becoming the flame of passion, burning deep in her belly and between her slowly moistening thighs.

When Christina finally stepped back Lianne wanted to cry out for her not to stop, for she was very near to orgasm, her nerve-ends shredded and desperate for release. Had it not been for the gag she knew she would have begged for the amazon to spank her to a climax – but Christina clearly had other ideas about that.

She nodded to Jodie, who evidently knew what was expected of her, for she reached into the packing-case and drew out a curious leather harness, from which hung a phallus complete with enormous testicles, all made from pure white leather and rubber.

Christina stood with legs apart and arms folded whilst Jodie strapped the harness onto her, fastening the cock and balls so that they projected from her loins like a huge erection. When the last strap had been adjusted Jodie stood aside, and Christina advanced on Lianne once again.

'I am told you adore being fucked whilst you are bound,' she hissed. 'Well, my cock may be a little different from that of any man who has had you, but it is just as effective and has more stamina. Jodie, remove her gag if you please.' When Jodie had done so Christina inched forward, pressing the tip of the dildo against Lianne's slit, where her clenched thighs were compressing it backwards towards the dominatrix. The entrance was already wet; Lianne's juices coating her pouting lips, but Lianne could not believe the woman could penetrate her with her legs so tightly closed. She felt the cold rubber probing insistently at her opening and gritted her teeth... But it seemed Christina was in no hurry. She placed her gloved fingers on Lianne's sore buttocks and squeezed them gently.

'Is this what you want, my little slave?' she crooned. Lianne groaned, for she knew it was what she wanted. The statuesque blonde stood motionless, even her hands no longer moving. 'Answer my question,' she said relentlessly.

Again Lianne groaned. '*Yesss*!' she gasped desperately.

'Yes what?' she heard Christina demand.

Lianne shuddered, tensing against her bonds. 'Yes, mistress,' she gasped. 'Yes... please... *mistress*!'

Satisfied with the response, Christina thrust forward and penetrated Lianne's vagina with surprising ease and filled her with one long stroke. Lianne cried out – but it was not a cry of protest, and as Christina began pumping in and out of her, her cries of delight became louder and wilder.

Separated from the poolroom by only a plasterboard

partition wall, Paul could hardly fail to hear the noise Lianne was making. Forgetting about his shackled ankles and not caring about the retribution such an action was sure to bring from Marika, he tried to spring up from the stool, and would have fallen had the girl not caught him. She thrust him back onto the stool unceremoniously and slapped his face.

'Any more of that and I'll take the whip to you,' she threatened, but Paul hardly heard her.

'What's going on in there?' he demanded. 'What are they doing to her?'

Marika gave him a cruel smile. 'Just setting a few standards for you to follow, I should imagine,' she said. 'Now, keep your mouth shut, or you'll be in serious trouble.'

From beyond the partition Lianne's shrieks grew louder and shriller until, after one ear-splitting cry, everything suddenly fell silent again.

Paul slumped on his seat, feeling utterly defeated and very stupid. If only they had not captured Lianne, he thought wretchedly, he could have refused to cooperate at all, but the prospect of her being returned to the depths of the pool was too awful to contemplate. He sighed and closed his eyes in resignation. Patience, he told himself. Patience and watchfulness; the bastards would make a mistake – sooner or later.

When Lianne was released from the bar, even though the leather sheath about her legs was removed, there was no way she could walk unaided; her knees were weak and trembling. Laughing at her predicament, the statuesque Christina eventually scooped her up and carried her across to the sturdy upright post, securing her to it initially by means of a broad strap, which she buckled about the helpless girl's waist. Satisfied that her captive would remain approximately upright, the Dane moved behind her and began unlacing the single sleeve that held her arms together. Lianne heaved a sigh of relief as the tension was released.

But her arms were not left free for long, for Christina hauled them above her head and secured them to straps set into the post for just that purpose. Jodie, who seemed able to read Christina's thoughts, stepped forward and passed her a long steel tube, at each end of which was another leather strap. Looking down, Lianne recognised the spreader bar, but her legs were still too weak to resist as they were drawn wide apart and secured to either end of it. Lianne felt her body sag a little, sliding through the waist strap and increasing the tension on her arms as her straddled position initially lifted her feet clear of the floor. However, when she had settled, the inside of each sole was making just enough contact with the stone to take most of her weight.

The collar was still in place about Lianne's neck, the chain leash hanging down her back. Christina unclipped the leash and, taking two finer, shorter lengths of chain from Jodie, attached them both to a ring at the front of the collar, where they dangled down just into the valley between Lianne's distended breasts. Christina paused, studying Lianne's eyes for any reaction that would indicate she knew what was coming next. Then very deliberately, she weighed Lianne's left breast, lifting it and molding it gently in her hand. Lianne stared back at her, willing her face to remain impassive, even though she had guessed the woman's intentions.

Sure enough, after a few seconds Christina lifted the

fleshy globe, took one of the chains, and clipped it to the nipple ring. The process was repeated on the other breast, and now a new fire began to spread through Lianne's body.

Christina stepped back, admiring her handiwork. 'How does that feel, my lovely slave?' she asked. Lianne looked into her steely eyes and was unsettled by what she saw there. The woman was a genuine sadist; this was no part she was playing for the cameras, this was really how she was. She clearly enjoyed inflicting pain on people who were in no position to resist. She reached out and slapped the outside of each of Lianne's tormented breasts in turn, jerking them against the already painful pressure of the rings.

'I said,' she hissed, 'how does that feel?'

Lianne gasped, trying to catch her breath. 'It hurts, mistress,' she croaked. 'It hurts a lot.'

'Good,' Christina said, stroking her sculptured jaw thoughtfully. 'Slaves should be subjected to pain, though the pain should also lead to pleasure. I was told that you enjoyed taking your pleasure through pain. Is that so?'

Lianne hung her head, avoiding the other woman's eyes. 'Not like this, mistress,' she whispered. But already Lianne knew she was fighting an awful truth, for her body was responding to the pain and humiliation in ever increasing degrees. Much more, she knew, and she would be begging for release, though not from her bondage, but from the screaming frustration that was damming up inside her even as she hung in her chains. Christina put one hand beneath Lianne's chin, lifting her face, so that she was forced to look into her eyes again.

'"Like this" is now your future, slave,' she said. '"Like this" and in any other way we decide. And if your new master's judgement – and mine – is correct, before long you will crawl on your hands and knees to submit to anything and everything.' She lowered her hand, her roughened fingers pressing against Lianne's excited sex lips. Lianne's eyes closed and she began to make little mewling sounds, tiny tears forming beneath each eyelid.

'That will do, thank you Christina.' The sound of James Naylor's voice jerked Lianne back to earth with a desire-crushing thud. She opened her eyes again as Christina backed away and, despite her predicament, it was all she could do to prevent herself from laughing out loud, for Naylor stood before her, clad in a pair of skimpy leather shorts, over which his paunch drooped heavily. His legs were sheathed in long, cavalry officer style boots, and a leather half-mask covered the upper part of his face and head. About his throat was a studded leather collar and his wrists were banded with smaller versions of the same. It was an outfit that was designed to strike terror into his victim, but the overall effect, primarily because of his stomach, was simply comic. However, the little multi-stranded whip that he clutched in his right fist was no laughing matter, and it was clear that the man took himself seriously.

'Well now, just look at the little slave girl,' he sneered. 'Legs wide open and just gagging for it.' He swished the whip through the air, the leather thongs whistling dangerously close to Lianne's left nipple. She cringed, but there was nowhere to go. Naylor smiled at her reaction. 'Don't try to kid me, sister,' he drawled. 'Remember, I saw your performances back at Nadia's. You just couldn't get enough, now could you? And it didn't seem to matter who with, either. Even Dean's leather lady routine had you begging for it long before you realised it was a man inside that suit.'

He flicked the whip again, and this time the tips of the thongs licked viciously against her distorted nipple, wrenching an involuntary squeak from her.

'That's better,' he said. 'I was beginning to think you'd lost your tongue. Or maybe you don't think I'm good enough for you, is that it?' He stung the other nipple with similar results. 'I suppose you think that good old Paulie is more your style, huh? Well, we'll see about that. That creep is a closet transvestite masquerading as a man.'

'I'd rather have that than a creep with a beer gut!' Lianne blurted, regretting the outburst immediately. Four times, backhand and forehand, the thongs snaked out, much harder than the first two blows and making Lianne feel as if her breasts were on fire. She gritted her teeth, trying to stifle her cries, but when the whip cracked against flesh for the fifth time, squarely between her open thighs, she let out a shriek of undisguised agony.

'Creep with a beer gut, eh?' Naylor goaded. 'Well, we'll see about that. Before I'm finished you'll be pleading with me to screw you.'

Lianne fought back the tears. 'Never!' she gasped. 'Hell will freeze over first.'

'We'll see about that,' Naylor rasped. 'And so will your new girlie partner.' He turned and called out towards one of the doors set in the wall behind the semi-circle of seats. 'Bring the new one out here!' he shouted. Immediately the door swung open and two figures emerged. The first, Marika, led the second on a chain that was attached to her collar.

Blinking furiously to clear her vision, Lianne stared at the approaching couple, wondering who the unfortunate maid was and whether she had been coerced like her. The girl was dressed in a parody of a French maid's outfit and was swaying on tall heels with every step, her stride restricted even more by the short hobble chain between her ankles. Her arms were behind her back, probably her elbows strapped together too, for she walked with her generous bosom thrust forward as though she were proud of her bondage and the gag which filled her mouth.

The pair came to a halt just to one side of Naylor, who looked from them to Lianne and back again. The lovely Asian girl stood relaxed, the chain slack in her hands, apparently confident of her control over her charge, whilst the maid's eyes darted agitatedly from side to side. It was only when they finally settled on Lianne and she saw the deep shame there that the terrible truth dawned on her – the maid was none other than Paul!

She stared at him in awed fascination, for he was barely recognisable under the transformation that Marika had wrought. In fact, so effective was the disguise of wig, makeup and padding, that anyone who had never met him before would almost certainly have been fooled into thinking he was a real woman. The only real clue was his height, but with so many tall females about even that was not giving away much.

'Meet Pauline,' Naylor said, laughing. 'She's your new heroine partner and she's come to watch you learn how to be a real slave. Of course, she's a slave now too.' As he spoke Christina stepped forward and whispered something in his ear. Naylor seemed to consider for a moment, his expression intent, but then a slow smile spread across what Lianne could see of his face. Behind the mask his eyes glittered maliciously.

'Yes,' he said slowly. 'An excellent idea. But first we must liven up our little hanging basket here.' He closed in again, whip raised. Behind him Paul made a move forward, but was brought up abruptly as Marika jerked viciously on his chain leash. For a second Lianne thought he was going to overbalance, but he regained his equilibrium just in time.

Paul's problems, however, were soon banished far from Lianne's thoughts as Naylor began to whip her, alternating between her nipples and her crotch and inner thighs. He struck slowly, methodically, and with unerring accuracy. Every stroke was like a dagger thrust, and Lianne jerked and swayed in her bonds as each one fell to the accompaniment of her shrieks and howls. And yet, despite the searing pain, each fresh fall of the lash was beginning to touch on some deeply submerged key and turning a lock that would soon open a secret, unknown chamber of her soul.

Her breathing was becoming faster and shallower, each gasp a tortured plea. She tried to speak, tried to beg, willing to promise anything to anyone, knowing that at any moment she would explode, debasing herself in front of so many knowing, eager eyes.

'Nooo!' she howled, thrusting her distended breasts forward in convulsive abandon. 'Nooo!'

And suddenly the whipping stopped, though the burning fires continued to blaze as she hung limply by her wrists, head lolled forward. She peered up through heavy lids, vision blurred by the tears that streamed down her cheeks, dripping onto the rubber and running onto the hot flesh of her heaving breasts. Naylor had moved aside, the whip hanging from his limp hand, and Marika was unbuckling the gag and removing it from Paul's mouth.

162

He spat the ball out and started to say something which Lianne could not make out, before another violent yank on the lead cowed him into silence.

'Kneel, slave Pauline,' Marika commanded. Jodie appeared at her side to pass her a leather riding crop, and Marika dealt Paul a hefty swipe across the back of his thighs to emphasise her order. Wincing, he struggled to obey, hampered as he was by his high heels and the fact that he could not use his arms to aid his balance. Another tug on the leash and another cut from the crop, this time across his shoulders, and he began to shuffle forward, stopping only when his face was a few inches from Lianne's burning sex.

'Satisfy the salacious tart,' Marika snapped and brought the crop down hard across Paul's buttocks, the crack as it struck the rubber of his skirt piercing Lianne's ears and making her cry out for him. Slowly Paul moved his face ever closer. His red lips parted and then his mouth was on her, his tongue probing. She felt her bud swelling as it was sucked into his mouth, the rough skin of his tongue massaging it rapidly with little darting strokes that stoked her furnace near to melting point. And then she was coming. She was climaxing in a frenzy of abandonment, not caring that they were all watching her, no longer even aware of their presence. Even the she-male apparition between her thighs faded into the mist and the lights and the stars that swirled around her until finally, blissfully, exhaustedly, the velvet blackness flowed up to claim her.

Just how long she remained unconscious, Lianne could not tell. It was probably not very long, for as her senses returned and she opened her eyes, she saw that the feminised Paul was still on his knees, though he had moved a few feet to one side and his gag had been replaced.

Naylor now stood in front of her with his leather shorts gaping and his erect penis clutched in his right fist. Lianne's eyes flickered from him to Paul and back again, registering the pained look in Paul's eyes and sensing the aura of helplessness that surrounded him. No doubt, had he not been so severely restrained, he would have leapt at Naylor and, in a fair contest, there would only have been one outcome – of that Lianne was sure.

She turned her head again, not wanting to look at Naylor, wanting to call out to Paul that it would be all right, for to her astonishment, there could be little doubt that her plight was wrenching him apart. She thought back to the day before yesterday to the moment when she had realised that it was him in the leather cat woman outfit, his cock sheathed in her hot, damp, welcoming tunnel. It had not been a tender coupling, but there had been something between them as the ritual had reached its shattering climax and she guessed that the thought of another man possessing her was more than Paul Dean could bear. Naylor evidently thought so to, for after allowing a few seconds for their eye contact to mature, he began taunting the rubber skirted prisoner.

'Not so clever as a girl now, are we Pauline?' he sneered. 'No cock to spring out and surprise the little lady today.' He turned back to Lianne. 'How's your lover girl going to satisfy you now, eh?' he demanded. 'Only with her tongue, like any other tart. And we all know how much you crave man-meat, girlie, don't we? Show her, Marika. Let the whore see how useless poor Pauline is now!'

Marika jerked the lead and Paul stumbled to his feet. The Asian girl dragged downwards on the chain, forcing him to arch his body backwards and then, with her free hand, she lifted the hem of his brief skirt. Lianne stared in horror and cried out in alarm, for where she had expected to see the bulge of his manhood there was nothing other than a smooth mound beneath the black rubber panties.

Naylor laughed a harsh, raucous sound. 'What do you think of her now then?' he cackled. 'Miss Pauline no-cock, the dutiful little maid.'

'Bastards,' Lianne hissed, her anger swamping the whole company. 'You evil bastards. What have you done to him?'

Naylor laughed again and even the straight-faced Marika smiled. Christina, who was lounging on the arm of one of the chairs, raised a hand to conceal the lower half of her face. With a pounding heart Lianne looked from one to the other and then beyond to Jodie, perched on the edge of one of the crates and the two men, who were leaning against the far wall. She began to wail, but the sounds died in her throat as she realised they were all finding the situation highly amusing. She looked back at Paul and he shook his head, quickly giving her a reassuring wink.

Once again she fixed Naylor with a malevolent look, fighting to stop her voice from shaking. She took a deep breath. 'You bastards,' she said again. 'Okay, you've had your little joke and I hope you're all satisfied.' She realised her voice was coldly calm now as a calculated hatred took control of her. 'Do your worst, you pot-bellied pig,' she told Naylor. 'You can call me what you want and I won't deny it. It's all true – every word of it.

If you screw me I'll probably get off on it the same as I would with anyone else. To a slave, one cock's as good as another. What are you waiting for, Jimmy?' she taunted him. 'That cock's not going to get any bigger, no matter how much you play with it. Why don't you put it in me and get it over with? That's what I'm here for, isn't it? I was a lucky break for you, so make the most of it. Come on Jimmy, or would you rather beat me again first? Where's your little whip?' She saw Christina pick up a ball gag from the armchair and begin moving towards her, but Naylor also saw it and raised a hand, halting the statuesque blonde in her tracks.

'Let her be,' he snarled. 'She can be as cocky as she likes, it just makes it all the more enjoyable. You can gag her afterwards and she can watch while you give Pauline what you gave her earlier. Of course Pauline will be a tighter fit, seeing as she's only got the substitute hole, but that's all part of the fun.' He turned back to Lianne, who had fallen silent but was breathing heavily. 'Got any more insults for me?' he said. 'I'm storing them all up for later, and you'll wish you'd kept your mouth shut, believe me.'

Lianne gave him a withering look. 'If you intend sticking that thing in me,' she said, 'you'd better hurry up. I don't want you spilling your load before you've satisfied me, now do I?'

Naylor grinned at her. 'No chance of that, girlie,' he retorted, moving towards her. 'No chance at all.' He stepped up, guiding his veined erection towards her helpless opening, and she felt the hot flesh nestling between her wet labia.

'You're nothing but a walking dildo to me,' she whispered, so quietly that nobody else in the room could hear her. She closed her eyes and sighed as he lifted his hips and sheathed his length inside her. She wondered why her body, despite everything and the fact that she could not have detested another human being more than she detested James Naylor at that moment, should already be responding to the fact that his shaft was sliding faster and faster in and out of her well-oiled sex.

She groaned, for unless Naylor was prone to serious premature ejaculation problems, she knew she was going to come well before him.

CHAPTER TWENTY

To Lianne's surprise, she and Paul were put in a room together. It was another cell-like room; a featureless rectangle two doors away from where she had first been kept. She was even more surprised that they were not left gagged, though they were chained by their collars to separate beds a few feet apart. They waited for several seconds after the door had closed behind the three women handlers before either of them risked speaking. It was Paul who broke the silence, though he only just pipped Lianne to it.

'How the hell did you get here?' he demanded. Lianne explained, careful not to omit any details, including what she had learned about Ellen switching the contents of the cases. Despite their predicament that amused Paul greatly.

'Clever girl, that one,' he said and, to her astonishment, Lianne felt a pang of annoyance that he should single

167

out her friend for commendation.

'Yes she is, but not that clever,' Lianne said sulkily. 'Though I should have thought about there being another man along, I suppose,' she admitted. 'What about you? Did they hurt you?'

'I got a crack on the back of the head,' Paul told her, 'but it wasn't really much. He just caught me off guard. I was a bit dazed and felt a bit sick, but the annoying thing is I probably could have got away while he was fetching the bloody cuffs. I never thought for one moment he'd come back. I didn't have a clue who he was at that stage. All I knew was he was wearing that damned suit of mine.'

'I guess he just panicked,' Lianne suggested. 'Though he seems to have turned the situation to his advantage. Do you reckon he'll try to keep us here for much longer?'

'I'm afraid that's almost certainly what he intends,' Paul replied quietly. 'I don't know where this place is, but it's certainly pretty remote – possibly as remote as Nadia's place. And Nadia can't even risk calling in the police, because though she's not doing anything illegal, the publicity would wreck everything she's built up.'

'Surely she's got contacts who would have heard something?' Lianne said. 'After all, Naylor's obviously spent quite a bit of time and trouble setting this operation up and running, and I should think he must have used some of Nadia's sources to get his equipment. And what about Christina? She'd hardly blend in with the average crowd, not unless they were all basketball players.'

'Maybe not, but she's a new face to me and I know most of the people on the so-called circuit. At a guess, I'd say Jimmy recruited her from abroad – either Holland or Germany. As for the other two, while they were almost certainly from this country to begin with, judging by the way they all work as a team, I'd be willing to bet they came as part of the same package.'

'So we're sunk,' Lianne said, her voice betraying the helplessness she felt. Paul pursed his bright red lips and shrugged.

'Not necessarily,' he said. 'No scheme's ever foolproof.'

Lianne brightened a little. 'Have you got a plan then?'

Paul smiled, sadly, she thought. 'Not as yet,' he admitted. 'But something will come up, you'll see. I intend to make Naylor pay for what they've done to you.'

'And you,' Lianne reminded him. She could not get out of her mind the picture when Christina had strapped her dildo on again and made him kneel on all fours, lifting up his skirt and taking him from behind, the white shaft sliding easily through the narrow slit in his rubber panties. She had wrapped one hand around him, the palm of her hand working between his thighs, pressing upon his trapped genitals, her attentions clearly having the desired effect on him, for the way he had buckled and fallen forward was a sure sign that he had climaxed. She looked at him, her gaze directed towards his loins.

'Does it hurt?' she asked. 'Having your bits scrunched up like that, I mean.'

'It did at first,' he admitted, 'but it's just gone sort of numb now.'

'I was nearly sick when they lifted your skirt the first time,' Lianne told him. 'I really thought they'd castrated you.'

'No, they wouldn't do that,' Paul assured her. 'From the way Naylor was talking, my "bits" as you call them are an essential part of his future action plans.' He told Lianne what he knew about Naylor's intention of using the Internet as a means of distribution. 'I have to admit,' he said, 'that he could be onto a winner. He did suggest it before, to me and Nadia, but that was a long time ago and the Net was still in its infancy.'

'I don't really know much about computers,' Lianne said. 'I used one for keeping appointments at the surgery, but that was just filling in little boxes. A trained monkey could have done it almost as well.' She looked across at Paul. 'I wish they'd chained us to the same bed.'

He smiled at her. 'You wouldn't mind sharing a bed with me looking like this?'

Lianne smiled back. 'Listen,' she said, 'I don't know what's happened to me these past few days, but I've found out things about me I neither understand nor would ever have believed possible. I've shared sexual experiences with total strangers and women, and I'm ashamed to admit it's been one big turn-on. I even had an orgasm with that bastard Naylor.'

'No need to be ashamed,' Paul said softly. 'The blonde bitch made me come, too.'

'I thought so. It must be feeling pretty uncomfortable by now.'

'I'll live,' Paul said. He considered for a moment. 'Doesn't it turn you off, seeing me like this?'

Lianne lay back against the single pillow. 'Why should it?' she questioned. 'You make a pretty convincing girl, and you do have one great advantage over the other girls I've met lately.'

'And you're not mad at me for the stunt with the cat woman outfit?'

'If ever we get out of this,' Lianne promised him, 'I'm

gonna have you back in that suit and you're gonna stay in it for a week. By the time I've finished with you, you'll feel like you've been spayed.'

'You mean neutered,' he corrected her. 'Spaying is for females.'

Lianne arched her eyebrows. 'I know what I mean – Pauline,' she said, her smile wider than ever.

CHAPTER TWENTY-ONE

Nadia ceased her pacing back and forth and turned hopefully at the sound of the lounge door opening. However, one look at the expression on Simon Prescott's face was enough to dash any optimism.

'No luck, I take it?' Nadia said. Simon shook his head, hopelessly.

'Whatever they're up to, they've covered their tracks well. I had Georgie Phillips check out Naylor's flat, but it's empty. It's up for sale, but the estate agents won't release any details of the vendor. All they would say was that they were selling it under instructions from a solicitor, acting on behalf of the present owner. Nothing on your famous grapevine, I suppose?'

'Nothing useful. There are rumours that someone's getting together something big, which they're intending to launch on the Internet, but no details. The Schwartz woman confirmed that she's supplied some girls to an organisation employing some Scandinavian dominatrix she knows slightly. Apparently the girls were all rejected, for various reasons she wouldn't go into.'

'Couldn't she find out where her girls went?'

'I already thought of that. It seems each of them was collected from a rendezvous point and driven to the ultimate destination in the back of a blacked-out van. They were returned the same way, so none of them has the faintest idea of where they were. All they could say was that it was about an hour and a half by road from South London, which doesn't narrow it down very much.'

'Any of them mention anything that would point to Naylor being involved?' Simon suggested.

'No, only this big blonde Scandinavian,' Nadia replied. 'Apparently, she's built like the side of a house and gets a bit too serious in her work. If she hadn't rejected the girls, I'm told they'd have quit anyway.'

'Then we're stuck. One, we don't have a clue where this place is and two, we don't even know if it's the right set-up.'

'I'm positive it's the one,' Nadia said firmly. 'I just feel it. And I'm not ready to just give up, either. I've got plenty of contacts on the continent. Schwartz says this Christina wanted more girls, but she was struggling to find suitable candidates. The woman apparently then told her she'd find her own recruits and she mentioned something about Germany or Holland, and said she could get "real" slaves for half of what Schwartz was asking anyway.'

'And you know someone who supplies these "real" slaves?'

Nadia smiled at him grimly. 'No,' she said, 'but I know a man who does.'

CHAPTER TWENTY-TWO

Lianne and Paul's quiet conversation was interrupted by the arrival of Marika and Jodie, the latter carrying a leather sack, which she dropped on the floor between the beds. Without a word they quickly gagged their victims.

'Time for a little light diversion,' the Asian girl announced. 'Christina's having herself a bath and something to eat, but we're getting bored, aren't we Jodie?' The curly brunette hair bobbed in confirmation. 'Right then, let's have the girlie-boy first.'

Alert as he was to the possibilities of trying to escape, Paul was given no chance by the two women. Neither was as powerful as the mighty Christina, but neither was a weakling either. His hands were released one at a time and cuffed to a broad leather belt which they locked around his waist, and then his left ankle was unlocked and hobbled to his right ankle before the latter was freed from the bed-frame. They did not have to exercise such precautions in Lianne's case, for she knew she was no match for the two of them. They quickly restrained her in the same way they had Paul, except they did not bother with the ankle hobble.

'Right, on the floor and on your knees,' Marika barked at Lianne. Lianne stumbled to obey. 'Head down, forehead on the floor.' Lianne leaned forward, placing her rubber-covered forehead on the hard stone. Looking backwards, she watched as Jodie reached up under

Paul's skirt and began dragging the rubber panties down his thighs.

'They won't come right off unless I unlock his ankles, Rika,' the girl complained. Marika shrugged.

'Don't bother,' she said. 'Leave them around his knees. It'll make things even more interesting. Right, that'll do. Get him nice and hard while I lubricate this one.'

Opening the bag that Jodie had brought with them, Marika took out a white jar and unscrewed the top. Dipping her fingers into its greasy contents, she stooped down and worked her fingers roughly between Lianne's buttocks, parting them and probing at her puckered ring. Lianne groaned to herself as she realised exactly what was intended, but she could not prevent the slippery digits from sliding inside and working the lubricant well into her rear passage.

Behind her Jodie announced that Paul was ready, lifting his skirts to reveal the rigid result of her ministrations. Marika straightened up and turned to him.

'You, my dear Pauline,' she sneered, 'are going to bugger this whore until one, or both of you, comes. And just to give you some encouragement,' she added, bending down to rummage in the sack again, 'I've brought this along.' She brought out a vicious looking cat o'nine tails and flicked it through the air with practiced expertise. 'Now, on your knees Pauline, and let's have some fun. Jodie, you guide his cock for him.'

Lianne tensed as she felt the first warmth of his shaft pressing against her and her first reaction was to resist it with all her might. However, Marika was not in the mood to be defied. The dark girl bent close to Lianne's face and brought the whip down hard on the stone floor just beside her. The sharp crack made Lianne jump and the diversion made her momentarily lose her muscular control. In that instant the head of Paul's cock eased its way just inside her. Marika was not prepared to take any chances though.

'Let him in,' she hissed, 'or I'll whip the skin off his prick!' With a whimper Lianne forced herself to relax and, slowly but surely, the hot shaft sank into her. She closed her eyes, biting hard on the ball gag. From behind her she heard the first slap of the leather thongs cutting into Paul's thighs, the impact forcing him deeper still.

'Fuck her!' Marika shrieked and the whip slashed home again. Paul had no option but to obey. With slow rhythmic strokes he pistoned in and out, and now the first pain of penetration began to give way to a different sensation. Lianne could feel her sex getting wetter and wetter and her heart and lungs began working overtime as she rose inexorably to another climax.

But Marika was having none of that – yet. She yelled to Paul to stop and then the two women helped the pair of them to their feet, still coupled together.

'You suck her, Jodie,' she instructed, breathing heavily. 'I'm going to fuck a pretty maid… all in a row.' She was scrabbling in the sack again and this time she pulled out a wicked looking double dildo, complete with a harness. Without ceremony she ripped open the crotch cover on her outfit and thrust one end of the beast into herself, hurriedly fumbling with the securing straps. Jodie was already on her knees before Lianne, her lips hungrily searching out her sensitive bud. Lianne gasped and heard Paul gasp too, and knew that Marika's cock was nudging against his rear opening, and then he groaned through his gag as she entered him.

'Stop whining, Pauline,' Marika sneered. 'You're hardly a virgin. Ah yes… that's better. The pumping rhythm started all over again, but by now Lianne was beyond all caring. As her throbbing clitoris was sucked into Jodie's eager mouth, she began the first of what was to be several mighty orgasms, all rolling into one in an extended surrender to her bodily lusts.

CHAPTER TWENTY-THREE

'It would appear that you really are a tart,' Christina said. Lianne was on her knees. The blonde amazon was standing over her, having just laced Lianne's arms into the single sleeve behind her back. The chains had remained on her breasts since her ordeal in the barn and there did not seem to be any immediate prospect of them being removed. At least the pain they had caused when the freezer spray had first worn off had dulled now to nothing more than a mild throbbing sensation, and it was more the ignominy of having those symbols of her womanhood so cruelly adorned that made Lianne wish they were gone. On the other hand, she was honest enough to admit to herself that the new look they gave her breasts, together with all the rubber, did make her feel deliciously wanton and somehow the combination of her appearance and her treatment released her from any sense of conscience. She stared up at the dominatrix, her face impassive.

'It would appear,' Christina was saying, 'that you are so depraved that the slightest touch, whether from a man or a woman, is enough to make you lose all self-control. You are a depraved whore, whose only thought is for her own sexual gratification.' That, thought Lianne, was a bit rich, coming as it did from one of her chief tormentors, but there was also more than an element of truth in her accusation. Three or four days ago Lianne would never have dreamed that sex with a virtual stranger, let alone sex with someone who would treat her so off-handedly cruel, could produce the sort of mind blowing orgasms she had repeatedly experienced.

Something had happened to her during that first afternoon on the estate, only minutes after she had first been rendered helpless. It was as though the chains and the straps had transferred all thoughts of moral responsibility and guilt completely away from her and, ever since, the centre of her being had moved from her brain to a spot somewhere far lower down. Even now, kneeling helplessly in front of this cold-hearted amazon, Lianne could feel the deep-seated yearning gnawing away at her like an empty stomach that has been deprived of food for days on end.

'Therefore,' Christina continued, 'I have decided that you need to be taught a lesson.' Memories of the pool flashed through Lianne's mind and she shuddered. That was the one experience she dreaded repeating and she knew that this woman knew it too. 'You will remain in your present bondage for the next twenty-four hours, during which no one will touch you sexually, neither between your legs, nor on your breasts or nipples. You will also wear a leather corset over what you have on now, laced as tightly as I can manage. So tightly in fact, that even breathing will be uncomfortable.

'You will also be put into a pair of boots that will

prevent you from walking – indeed, even standing up in them will require a great deal of effort and help from someone else. This means you will remain on your knees, crawling everywhere, like the little worm that you are.

'During this punishment period you will not be idle, for there are six of us here whom you will service on a regular basis, using that pretty little mouth of yours. At the end of the twenty-four hours you will be permitted to remove all your present clothing and bathe, after which I have a new outfit, especially for lascivious little nymphomaniacs. Once it is in place neither you, nor anyone else, will be able to give you any sexual stimulus at all. Master James and I will hold the only keys.'

The corset was a fearsome looking creation made from thick black leather, heavily boned and designed to encompass a waist much smaller than Lianne's own. As Christina began loosening its laces, Lianne was convinced the garment would never go around her, but go around her it did, Christina using every ounce of her awesome muscle power to draw the two halves together and fasten them at the front. Lianne gasped for air, determined not to plead for clemency, for she knew none would be forthcoming. But there was worse still to come, for now the awesome blonde turned her attention to the laces at the back.

Despite the handicap of having to work around Lianne's bound arms, Christina relentlessly hauled on the thick cords, pushing Lianne face down on the floor and anchoring her with a booted foot planted strategically between her shoulder-blades and one knee prising her arms clear of her body. Inexorably, the gap between the two sides closed and Lianne felt herself becoming light-headed as the air was squeezed from her lungs.

'You'll have to get used to breathing more shallowly,' Christina said, at last tying off the laces. 'Small breaths, and don't rush it. You'll get the idea quickly enough.' She removed her boot from Lianne's back and used it to roll her victim over onto her side. Lianne lay motionless, only the slight rise and fall of her chest betraying that she was still alive as she fought to master the new way of breathing. To her relief she found that Christina was right and the dizziness began to subside as oxygen reached her brain again.

When Christina brought the boots Lianne just stared at them in disbelief, for if she had thought any of her previous footwear extreme, this was a different league. Made of black leather, they were knee length and had heels so high that the instep pointed straight down, only the blocked toes making any contact with the floor. As Christina forced Lianne's left foot into the first boot and began the arduous process of lacing it, Lianne realised that if she could stand at all in these bizarre creations, her feet would have to assume the classic *en pointe* position normally attempted only by trained ballerinas. This assumption was confirmed by Christina's next words.

'These are called ballerina boots,' she said. 'I have kept slaves in these for weeks at a time, as extra punishment for disobedience or insolence. I had one slave in Switzerland who was a classical dancer. She was the only one who ever managed to walk in them properly, though some of the others eventually managed to get around in them. It is quite remarkable what practice and perseverance can achieve, even if their progress was slow and ungainly. However, I do not think you will be running around in these just yet, though we will try you standing, just for a little while.'

She completed lacing the second boot and then effortlessly hoisted Lianne to her feet. As her weight went down Lianne thought her calf muscles must explode, and it was all she could do to prevent herself from overbalancing. She tottered, her feet arched unbelievably, until she finally found a stance, with her legs a few inches apart and her torso leaning slightly forward, where she could stay upright. But how long she would be able to maintain that position was another matter entirely.

Christina did not bother waiting to find out. From among the pile of things that lay to one side she drew out a riding crop, and delivered a sharp cut across Lianne's rump. Lianne staggered from the blow, and was unable to bend her knees in time to stop herself from slumping forward. Her knees hit the floor with a painful crack and her head banged into the uncompromising stone. She remained in that position, her buttocks thrust into the air, sobbing with the pain, the humiliation, and the anger that the woman's callous attitude had triggered. Under her breath she swore savagely, but the Dane allowed her little respite.

The crop slashed down again, drawing a scream of agony from Lianne as it unerringly cut into the exposed portion of her rump. Above and behind her, Christina laughed, mirthlessly.

'You stay on your knees now,' she said. 'And just to make sure, I have a few more decorations for you.'

She took out a set of steel ankle hobbles and locked them in place over the boots, locking another length of chain to the circular centre link. She then drew this second chain underneath Lianne's crouching form and secured it to the front of her collar, leaving just sufficient slack for Lianne to affect a crawling motion.

'Yes, I think you look suitably humble for a slave now,' Christina said. 'Just one final thing and you're ready.' Lianne was not especially surprised to see the ball gag being offered to her lips, and made no effort to resist as Christina pushed it into her mouth and buckled the strap tightly about her face.

Lianne's leg muscles were beginning to knot themselves into the first warning signs of impending cramp. Over an hour had elapsed since Christina had left her, still kneeling with yet another chain attached to her collar and clipped to a ring set in the floor. This was far worse than anything else they had inflicted upon her; being abandoned in her bondage, forgotten and unimportant. All the whips in the world, all the dildoes and the cocks, none of that held any terrors for her any more, for she knew now that all the pain and humiliation led to one road and one road only – the road of abandonment, with the ultimate of pleasures as its destination.

But Christina knew that too, it seemed, which was why she had selected this cruelest of all punishments for Lianne. She lay on the hard floor, legs bent, her right breast against the cold stone, and battled against the overwhelming urge to weep. She closed her eyes and thought back – back to the cat woman who had suddenly grown a penis. Back to Gavin, to Ellen, and to the cruel but glorious whipping she had received at the poolside. Throughout all of it she had endured, absorbed, demanded finally, and found a part of herself she had never suspected existed. Afterwards she had even rationalised her new situation, admitting to herself that it hardly mattered if the bondage were temporary or permanent, the scenario real or pretend, as long as the end result was the same. But now, chained and leashed, forced to crawl and grovel like the lowest dog, knowing there would be no personal release at the end of everything, Lianne was close to despair.

It was almost a relief when the door finally opened again, even though the sight of the huge Eric Raines was hardly the most reassuring thing Lianne could have hoped for. He stooped down beside her and reached out a hand. She cringed, but his touch was surprisingly gentle as he stroked her cheek.

'Poor little cow,' he said softly. 'That blonde bird is as mental as Jim, I reckon.' He reached behind her head and unbuckled the gag strap, easing the ball out of her mouth. Lianne swallowed and ran her tongue around her lips.

'Thank you,' she whispered. His face was expressionless, though his eyes looked troubled.

'If I'd known they were going to go this far,' he said, 'I'd have just tied you up and left you back there.'

'You could still let me go,' Lianne suggested hopefully. Eric shook his head.

'Even if I thought it worth the risk, I don't have the key. Christina keeps the one master key in a little pouch in that white outfit of hers. Even Jimmy doesn't have one.'

'*The* key?' Lianne gasped. 'There must be loads of keys. I mean, there are five locks just in this lot,' she said, nodding her head in an attempt to indicate her own bondage.

'Yeah, but they're all the same,' Eric told her. 'These little padlocks,' he fingered the one between her breasts,

182

'are part of a bulk load. I know, 'cause I drove to Sheffield to collect them. There must have been a couple of hundred of 'em in the box. They all had their individual keys, but I had to take 'em all out and give 'em to superbitch. I don't know what she did with 'em, but I've only ever seen the one. When she's wearing the white outfit, it slips into the little pocket thing. Other times she clips it to a chain around her neck. And besides the key problem, there's something else.'

'Money?' Lianne suggested. Again he shook his head. 'That's not that important,' he said. 'I mean, the pay's good, but it's not that. No, Jimmy's got something on me, from where I used to work. I – well, I sort of turned a blind eye to a scam that was going on in this big warehouse and Jimmy got hold of a video of me taking some money off the bloke who was organising it.'

'He's hardly going to take that to the police, is he?' Lianne said. 'After all, you could blow the whistle on him over all this lot.'

'Maybe I could, but it wouldn't help me. I was already on a two year suspended for thumping some bloke in a pub brawl, and I had previous for thieving and taking cars when I was a lad. The way the courts are coming down hard these days, I'd be looking at a five stretch.'

'From what they've been saying, I'm looking at more than that,' Lianne retorted bitterly. Eric spread his hand around the top of her arm, gripping it, though without any force.

'I could try talking to them,' he offered.

'And do you think that'd do any good?'

'No. No, it wouldn't,' Eric said, his voice sad. He released his hold on her and sat back on his haunches. 'I'm sorry,' he said. 'I really am.'

183

'And is that what you came in here for, to apologise? If so, then thanks very much, but apology not accepted.'

'I wouldn't expect it to be,' he said. 'No, I was told to come in here and get a blow job off you – my reward for catching you in the first place.'

'But you feel too guilty.'

'Something like that.'

'You mean it doesn't turn you on, the prospect of having a rubber slave girl suck your cock? You do surprise me!'

'Of course it'd turn me on,' Eric retorted. 'It'd turn on any bloke.'

'Then why don't you do it?'

Eric's eyebrows shot up. 'You mean you don't mind? No, you're having me on.'

'Why? Maybe I want to do it for you. Maybe I want you to screw me as well.'

'Jim and Christina said that was a no-go. They said just your mouth and not to touch you anywhere else.'

'Not even to touch my breasts?' Lianne purred. There was a glimmer of light flickering at the end of the tunnel now and she was desperate to keep it burning, even if it was a very small light and a very long tunnel. 'Help me kneel up,' she said. Eric hesitated, but only for a moment. He scooped her up effortlessly onto her knees. She looked up at him as he stood before her and smiled, though the mask was concealing most of her attempt.

'I'd appreciate something softer to kneel on,' she whispered sweetly. 'This floor is so hard.'

'What? Oh, yes.'

Lianne could tell her calmness was causing him a great deal of confusion. He looked around, searching for something to use, and eventually settled for an old sack that he folded into several thicknesses. 'Sorry, it's the best I can do,' he said, lifting her and pushing the rough hessian into position.

'It's not your fault,' Lianne said. 'And thank you.' Eric stood there, looking like a lost child at a football match. Lianne took a deep breath. 'Why don't you take your clothes off?' she suggested. He looked puzzled.

'All of them?'

She nodded. 'Yes, why not. I bet you've got a great body under there, and it's so much better if you're naked. Unless you're like me of course, and respond better to all this kinky gear.'

'No,' he said. 'At least, not for myself. It looks great on you, same as all the leather stuff does on those girls out there. But you're right – I prefer naked too.' He turned away and began peeling off his tee-shirt. Shoes, socks, trousers and briefs followed. When he turned back again Lianne had to stifle a gasp, for his penis, even in its flaccid state, was in proportion to the rest of his physique. She instinctively ran her tongue along her top lip.

'Are you sure you wouldn't rather put that somewhere other than my mouth?' she sighed coquettishly.

He crouched down before her and cupped her face between his massive hands. 'Sweetie,' he said, 'there's nothing I'd like more, but superbitch reckons she's going to check you over afterwards... Sorry.'

Lianne sighed again, the frustration welling up inside her. How could they possibly be so heartless? She could handle all the rubberwear and the bondage – in fact, in a very short space of time she had come to love it – but it was so unfair to deny her her own satisfaction after deliberately setting out to arouse her. That was nothing short of total wickedness. But that, Lianne now understood, was the difference between Nadia's set-up and the one that James Naylor headed here.

Eric stood up, his right hand gently massaging his organ, which was slowly beginning to respond. Lianne stretched her neck forward.

'Let me,' she urged softly, her moist tongue flickering invitingly. Eric was clearly uncertain about all this, for it seemed his huge frame hid a basically gentle nature. But he eventually shuffled close again and offered his swelling shaft to Lianne's mouth. Greedily she sucked the shiny purple knob between her lips, her tongue lapping over the sensitive flesh. She heard Eric grunt his pleasure and felt him shudder and knew it would not take long to bring him to his peak. She still did not fully comprehend this new world of pain and pleasure, bondage and servitude, but she knew she must present an exotically alluring sight in her chains and rubber, kneeling submissively before this giant of a man.

Lianne felt his fingers entwining themselves in her ponytail, but they did not exert any pressure on her, simply establishing a contact which, in its way, was almost as intimate as the one taking place between her stretched lips. Steadily, Lianne began to increase the pace of her oral ministrations, her head bobbing gently and, exactly as she had surmised, Eric could not restrain himself for long under such exquisite attentions. With a strangled cry he ejaculated, filling her mouth with a hot, salty jet. He followed the first one with two weaker efforts before he staggered backwards, knees buckling. Lianne swallowed gratefully and inhaled a lungful of air. She waited for him to recover his composure.

He did, but the look on his face was a strange one;

part desire, part guilt, part gratitude. He looked down at his rapidly deflating organ and turned away, snatching up his briefs. Lianne managed to suppress a smile.

'Was that satisfactory... master?' she enquired coyly. Eric turned his head, his eyes flickering uncertainly.

'What? Yes... thank you,' he mumbled stupidly. Lianne bowed her head submissively.

'No,' she said, 'thank *you*, master... It was all my pleasure, as well as my duty.'

Eric clumsily finished pulling on his underwear and stepped into his trousers, fastening the waistband and pulling up his fly zipper. He stepped back to Lianne and lifted her face.

'Do you really enjoy being tied up and doing things like that?' he asked incredulously. Lianne kept her face raised, but lowered her eyes to deliberately avoid his gaze.

'It depends on who I am doing it for,' she replied, choosing her words carefully. The light was burning slightly brighter now, though it was still a long tunnel. 'For the right master I can be the perfect slave – more than any man could ever dream of.' Eric let out a harsh breath and she could almost hear the cogs turning inside his brain.

'And what is your idea of the perfect master?' he asked. Lianne already had that answer prepared.

'A man who is strong, but not cruel. Hard, but also gentle and appreciative of his slave's efforts to please him.' She paused deliberately. 'I think you would be such a master,' she finished smoothly. He let her chin drop again and turned to scoop up his shirt.

'And you'd really be happy to spend your life in rubber and chains?'

'If the chains were not always as cruel as these,' Lianne said. 'And if my master would occasionally pleasure me, or at least let me pleasure him as a woman should.' He slipped the tee-shirt over his head, wriggled his stout arms through the short sleeves, and turned for the door.

'I'll see you again soon,' he said, his voice still unsteady. 'No promises mind, but I'll think about what I can do for you... And what you can do for me.'

As the door closed behind him the light grew brighter and slightly closer, and the tunnel did not seem quite so long.

CHAPTER TWENTY-FOUR

For the rest of the day Lianne alternated between periods of bored inactivity and sessions when she was called upon to satisfy the other men in the same way she had satisfied Eric. Naylor, in particular, seemed to take particular satisfaction in using her mouth, returning three times in the space of as many hours. It did cross Lianne's mind that her teeth could be used to inflict a painful and serious injury on him, but fear of the retribution such an action would bring, coupled with a horror of causing such harm to another human being, even Naylor, held her back.

Instead, she simply kept her eyes closed and concentrated on bringing him to the point of release as quickly as possible, remembering Ellen's words about being able to recognise something in a natural submissives eyes and knowing now that her friend's assessment of her nature had been uncannily accurate.

Eventually, after Marika had also availed herself of Lianne's services, she was given a bowl of scrambled eggs and a mug of coffee, her arms released so she could feed herself.

Christina came for her not long after that, clipping her leash to the collar and leading Lianne back out to the poolside area. Lianne's eyes darted about, looking for any sign of Eric, but he was not there. Tony the van driver was, having changed from his jeans and shirt into a leather outfit that was all straps and buckles, apart from a pair of leather briefs that did little to cover his bulging manhood. His eyes devoured Lianne greedily as she crawled in and it was obvious that her efforts with him earlier had done little to diminish his libido.

Paul Dean, still looking remarkably feminine in his maid's outfit, hung from the pole. His legs were spread wide by the bar, in exactly the same position Lianne had occupied earlier. His cheeks bulged around a large ball gag, but he tried to communicate with Lianne with his eyes. From beneath the brief hem of his dress Lianne saw a heavy looking weight hanging from a taut chain, and she flinched when she realised where the hidden end of the chain must be tethered.

Naylor occupied one of the chairs, lounging back, still in his ridiculous leather shorts and mask, a cigar in one hand and a glass of something dark in the other. Marika and Jodie stood waiting to one side, another packing-case open beside them. Naylor grinned widely as Lianne approached, transferring his cigar to his mouth and pointedly patting his groin.

'It's still hungry for you,' he leered. 'Are you still

189

hungry for *it*?' He laughed, the cigar bobbing up and down as he did. Looking at Christina, he said, 'Are you sure she didn't frig herself while her hands were free?'

Christina nodded with an air of absolute confidence. 'I'm sure,' she said.

Marika and Jodie stepped forward and Christina passed them the tiny key, which just as Eric had said, she produced from a little pouch on the hip of her leather costume. Marika quickly began releasing the locks, leaving Jodie to remove them and the various manacles and chains which they had been securing. The chains were then removed from Lianne's nipples and all the rubber stripped from her body.

'Throw her in the pool,' Christina ordered. 'And make sure she keeps her hands where you can see them.'

The cool water felt good and Lianne slowly paddled herself around, letting it gently wash the smell of rubber and perspiration from her body. After about ten minutes Christina ordered her to the side, where her two cohorts hauled her out of the soothing water. She was given a towel and allowed to dry herself, though her hair was still damp when Marika guided her over to the packing-case.

'I promised you a rare treat,' Christina said, 'and now you shall have it.' She half turned, looking at the case. Lianne followed her gaze and saw something metallic and shiny. In fact, there were quite a lot of things metallic and shiny. 'In here,' Christina continued, 'we have my latest innovation. I designed it myself and it has been made by one of the finest craftsmen in the world. It is, in fact, to be your new uniform, except when you are required to dress specifically for photo sessions.

'As I told you, I think you are only too ready to allow

yourself to be used. But slaves are not here for their personal gratification. Keeping your hands chained is all very well, but that prevents you from being useful between times. Slaves should also work properly for their keep, apart from their other uses. In days gone by lords left their ladies in chastity belts to prevent them being violated in their absence. I have taken the concept one step further. When you are dressed in this you will have no access to your sex, to your bottom-hole, or even to your breasts and nipples.

'There is a facility to enable you to use the toilet, but you will need one of us to unlock it and you will be accompanied to ensure you do not take advantage of the situation.' She nodded to Marika, who lifted the first item from the crate. Lianne stared, goggle-eyed, for the shiny steel had been molded into what looked exactly like a one-piece swimsuit, except that the cups that would cover her breasts were conical and pointed. Whilst Marika held it up Christina began releasing tiny lockable catches that ran up either side until the two halves, front and back, separated.

Lianne stood quietly as they began fitting the metal garment to her, the snap of each catch being eased home sounding louder than it really was. It was a slow, precise task, for the thing had been made to be a very tight fit and they had to take great care that her flesh was not pinched between the two halves. When they had finished there was an oval aperture revealing Lianne's vagina and anus, but it was not left open for long. A curved piece of steel was locked into the waiting catches and she was completely sealed, as promised, unable to touch any part of herself that might provide stimulation. Lianne stared down, totally mesmerised by the effect, for it was like being in one long corset, her stomach flattened by the unyielding steel, her breasts – or at least the steel which covered them – jutting out in two pointed cones. The steel crotch-piece pressed into the soft flesh at the inner creases of her thighs, forcing her to stand with her legs slightly apart. It was, she was forced to admit, a bizarrely sexy creation, but it was one piece that was designed purely for the benefit of the onlooker and definitely not for the wearer.

'I call this the *Steel Virgin*,' Christina told her. 'And when we have fitted the rest of it, I advise you to keep well clear from the pool. If you were to slip, or trip, you would sink like a stone.'

Lianne soon saw what the tall blonde meant. A wide steel collar was locked about her neck, followed by two arm-pieces that went about her forearms, stretching down to enclose her hands as far as the penultimate knuckle joint. With them in place she retained a restricted use of her hands, but her thumbs were completely enclosed and held rigidly, making any task which required real dexterity totally impossible.

The steel boots were thigh length, with no flexibility at the knee, and there was a chain connecting the two ankles which would restrict her stride to no more than eight or nine inches. When, at Christina's instruction, Lianne attempted to walk, she found she could barely lift her feet and was forced to adopt a stiff-legged, shuffling gait in order to make any progress. The boots felt even heavier than she had expected. Christina soon solved this mystery for her.

'Each sole and each heel has a lead insert,' she said. 'As I said, this outfit is for punishment and, on those occasions when you are released from it, you will learn

192

to be truly grateful.'

As she stood there feeling like a robot, Lianne thought they could do no more to her, but she was wrong. She had noticed the various semi-circular steel staples set into the steel bodice, and she had also seen those set into the inside of each arm-piece, but had not understood their significance. Now she did, as Marika locked the inside of each elbow to either side of her waist. The locks were cunningly designed to allow a certain amount of swivelling, in order that she might raise and lower her arms, but prevented any lateral movement, thus removing any threat of her using her steel covered arms as weapons.

'You will remain dressed like this for twenty-four hours,' Christina informed her.

Lianne's heart sank, for unless she had assistance, she could see no way in which she could get herself into any sort of position to rest. The only option would be a bed much higher than anything she had seen so far, for with her rigid legs and restricted arms, even if she did manage to get down, getting upright again would be an insurmountable challenge.

'You will also be punished for the amusement of your new master. Come!'

Christina clipped a chain leash onto Lianne's collar and dragged her across to the area immediately in front of the chairs, a few feet from where Paul hung helplessly from the post. Marika, meanwhile, had made her way across to the wall behind the chairs and flipped open the cover on a control panel. She operated one of the switches and, from high above in the rafters, a heavy chain began to descend. Looking up, Lianne saw that it was, in fact, several chains hanging from the end of one master chain and that each of the subsidiary chains terminated in a snap catch. When the whole assembly was low enough Christina began attaching these catches to the steel hasps on Lianne's outfit.

One went in the centre of her back, another to the back of her collar, and two more to links at the back of her knees. The final pair went to rings on the outside of her wrists and then the chain was moving again, this time in an upward direction. Before she had time to prepare herself, Lianne was jerked into the air, her upper body falling forwards until the chain from her collar halted the momentum. The chains at the back of her knees held her legs suspended in a straight line from her body. When Marika shut off the power Lianne was left hanging helplessly, face down, at an angle of about forty-five degrees to the floor, which remained tantalisingly just a few inches below her steel-shod feet.

Still not satisfied, Christina removed the hobble chain from between her ankles and replaced it with a spreader bar, which she further adjusted until Lianne's legs were stretched apart.

Putting down his cigar and glass, Naylor stood up. He reached behind his chair for an evil looking multi-thonged whip. Each of the braids was thick and looked as though it had been recently oiled, for the black leather shone ominously under the lights.

'As you can see,' he whispered coldly, 'your armour plate leaves plenty of you bare for me to thrash. I think we'll start here.' He stepped to one side and brought the whip flailing down across the top of Lianne's right thigh, several of the thongs cutting into the exposed flesh of her lower buttock too. She let out a scream of agony as the searing pain burned into her straining flesh, but

Naylor simply ignored her and aimed the second stroke across her right shoulder and upper arm. Again she screamed and thought she must surely faint.

Naylor walked around in front of her, raising the whip and placing the stock under her chin, forcing her head up.

'I don't know why we're even bothering with the whiz-kid's graphics,' he laughed. 'You already look like a cartoon character without them. All we have to do is animate you a little more.' He stepped around to her left side and repeated the same two strokes as he had given her on the right, only this time in quick succession. Lianne shrieked and thrashed as far as her bonds would allow, the chains creaking and rattling under her exertions.

'That's better,' Naylor gloated. He lifted her chin once more. 'I bet you'd rather suck my cock than take any more of this, wouldn't you?'

Lianne, her eyes full of tears, did not answer, and as a reward he dealt her two upward, backhanded slashes, catching the tender insides of the tops of her thighs. He ignored her wails, waiting until they had subsided into sobs.

'I asked you a question,' he said calmly. 'Or would you rather taste more of my little friend here?'

Lianne gulped. 'No...' she finally managed to gasp. 'No... master.'

Naylor leaned his head on one side, his eyes glinting behind the mask. 'You mean you don't want to suck my cock again?' he goaded.

Lianne shook her head desperately. 'No... I do,' she moaned. 'I mean yes... please let me suck your cock, master.' Anything, she thought, anything was better than the whip.

Naylor considered her for a while and then nodded, apparently satisfied.

'Lower her a little,' he ordered Marika, and the motor started up once more. Inch by inch, Lianne descended, her toes now just touching the floor, her head just above the level of Naylor's groin. Marika made a couple of fine adjustments, so that now the chains to her legs no longer took any weight, but now Lianne's face was at the ideal height. Dimly, through misted eyes, she watched as he opened the front of his leather shorts. His rigid erection sprang out ready for action. She closed her eyes and dutifully opened her mouth wide, waiting to receive it.

'You're learning fast,' she heard Naylor say, and then he stepped forward and fed his engorged helmet between her lips, not waiting for her to lick or suck him, but holding the back of her head with one hand and using the other to masturbate himself. Within seconds he came, filling her mouth and throat with his semen.

'Get her down and get her out of here,' Naylor ordered brusquely as he withdrew and turned away from her. 'Take her back to one of the cells. I'm going to amuse myself with her girlfriend here.' He jerked a thumb in the direction of Paul.

Christina stepped forward and supported Lianne's weight, levering her upright as Marika slackened off the chains. The spreader bar was removed, but she didn't bother with replacing the ankle chain, obviously confident that the heavy soles of the boots were restrictive enough. She refastened Lianne's leash and jabbed a finger into her upper arm, where the flesh was already bright red from Naylor's whip.

'Get moving,' she commanded. 'I'm going to chain you down on a nice comfortable bed, where you can have all night to recover yourself. Tomorrow I've got a few new ideas to try on you. I can't promise you'll like them very much, but then we're not worried about a slave's opinion, are we?'

Her flesh still burning, Lianne turned and began shuffling towards the door, where she had to wait until Christina turned the handle, before shambling outside into the yard. To her surprise it was still daylight and, to judge from the length of the shadows, there was still a couple of hours before sunset. The air felt cool, but all too soon Lianne was back inside the main house, deprived of its soothing touch on her inflamed skin.

They came to the cellar steps and Lianne hesitated. Behind her, Christina chuckled.

'What are you waiting for, slave?' she teased. 'Keep moving.'

'I – I don't think I can... mistress,' Lianne muttered nervously. 'It's these boots. I can't bend my knees.'

'Then put your feet together and hop down, one step at a time.'

Still Lianne hesitated.

'Move it, or I'll take my crop to you when we get downstairs.'

Steeling herself, Lianne placed her legs together and, drawing upon all her strength, managed to hop over the edge onto the first step down, her steel boots clattering and ringing on the bare stone. She edged forward and repeated the manoeuvre – and then again, and then again.

Quite how she made it to the bottom of the stairs without either overbalancing or collapsing from the effort, she didn't know, but finally she stood in the subterranean corridor, leaning against the wall and gasping for breath. This time it seemed Christina knew she could push her prisoner no further, for she simply watched quietly as Lianne slowly recovered what was left of her strength.

'We'll make a decent slave of you yet,' the tall blonde said, rattling Lianne's leash chain. 'And now if you're ready, it's time to move.' She nodded, indicating for Lianne to go left, the direction of the room in which she and Paul had spent the previous night. Resignedly, Lianne straightened up and began to move on.

As she did so a light suddenly flicked on in the foggy mass that, until a few seconds before, had been her brain. It was a desperate chance, she knew, but then what did that matter? After all, they had done just about everything to her that they could. What else could she be made to endure that would be worse than already endured? With calm deliberation she slowed her pace as much as she dared, trying to give herself the maximum time to recover every possible ounce of strength. She would need it.

They came at last to the door of her cell. Christina reached past her, turned the handle, and pushed against the door to open it. Lianne stepped forward immediately, for it was crucial that she entered the room in front of her captor. She let out a few wheezing, gasping sounds, anxious to distract Christina and to lull her into a false sense of security. Affecting to stagger even more than she might have normally done and lurching to her left, she ducked around the edge of the door.

From where the strength came she had no idea, nor how she managed to time the backward kick so accurately. Her weighted boot crashed into the heavy timber with so much force that it slammed against the unsuspecting Christina, cracking her squarely in the centre of her forehead. Lianne stumbled against the door and caused it to rebound, this time to strike the stunned blonde on the temple. Staggering to regain her balance, Lianne retained enough presence of mind to kick out again, her lethal boot smashing into Christina's shin with such force she heard the bone snap. Luckily for Christina she was already unconscious and felt no pain as she slid to the floor in an ungainly heap. For a few seconds Lianne stood transfixed, unable to believe she had actually done it, but then she snapped out of her trance and set about making the most of this new situation.

With great difficulty she managed to bend at the waist and fumble for the key in Christina's pouch, using the first and second fingers of her right hand, her thumb being completely useless. The two digits closed on the hard metal and she carefully withdrew it, determined not to let it slip, for if it fell to the floor there was no easy way she could recover it. Awkwardly she reached her right forearm across her body, probing for the articulated lock that held her other elbow close to her side. The key slid in easily enough, but when Lianne tried it it steadfastly refused to turn.

Desperately she transferred the key from one hand to the other and tried again on the right hand side. The result was the same. With a howl of frustration Lianne realised the truth. The single key operated all the small padlocks that were used in the general bondage equipment, but this outfit, by Christina's own words, was completely new. She staggered to the bed, dropped the useless key onto it and staggered back again, bending to feel into the tight pouch again, praying there would be another key there.

The pouch was empty. She used her boot to turn the recumbent dominatrix and examined her outfit for signs of another pocket on the other side, but there was nothing there, the smooth line of the white leather totally uninterrupted. She swore aloud and kicked the door in frustration, almost overbalancing in the process.

'Stop it!' she snapped out loud, and then made a conscious effort to calm herself. 'Stop it. Think, you stupid bitch... think...'

She bent over again and studied Christina's face, and was relieved to see there was no sign of an imminent return to consciousness. She looked around at the various restraints and gags hanging from their wall rack, but none of them were any use to her, not unless she could find a way of getting down to Christina's level, which the boots made impossible. She could reach the woman, but not quite far enough to put cuffs and a gag on her.

Lianne decided she would have to chance the fact that Christina would remain out cold for some while yet, but she certainly could not leave her where she was; half in and half out of the doorway. She turned back to the rack, searching for something she could use, and her eye fell upon a long leather leash with a heavy spring clip on one end of it. She shuffled across, took the strap down, and examined it closely.

She quickly decided there was no way she could operate the spring clip, not with her fingers so badly handicapped by the steel gloves, but another idea occurred to her at the same instant. Very carefully, she managed to thread the free end of the leash through the metal ring of the clip, drawing it through until she had a loop of leather which would have been about eighteen inches in diameter, had it been perfectly round. Holding the leather and steel between two fingers so that the loop could not yet tighten, Lianne returned to Christina. She wedged herself against the edge of the open door to assist her balance.

She extended her left foot, forcing it between Christina's right leg and the stone floor, and raised the woman's foot a few inches into the air. Bending forward, she then lowered the loop, passed it over the end of the boot, and released the clip, pulling upwards on the leash so the noose tightened around Christina's ankle. With a sigh of relief Lianne straightened, stepped back, and began wrapping the free end of the leather about her right wrist, adding turn after turn until she was sure it would not slip off.

Dragging the hefty amazon right into the room proved an exhausting task, the unconscious body moving scant inches at a time, but Lianne persevered and eventually got her into the space between the two beds, the nearer of which would partially obscure her from anyone entering. Uncoiling the leather from her wrist, Lianne let it fall to the floor and returned to the door where she peered out into the corridor and listened for any signs of movement. Satisfied everything was still quiet, she carefully closed the door, moved behind it, and slumped against the wall with a sigh of relief.

Time ceased to have any meaning as Lianne waited. Her head was full of jumbled thoughts and ideas, but she had no definite plan. She could try to make her escape, but the stairs had proved a big enough problem on the way down – getting up them would be well nigh impossible without some sort of help. She could perhaps try hiding in one of the other rooms, but that would be a pointless exercise, for they were bound to search and she would quickly be discovered. She needed the keys that would unlock the catches on her boots, but where they were she had no idea.

Finding a telephone would be one possibility. It would mean calling the police, for she had no idea of Nadia's number. But at least it would get her out of this place and all the questions and recriminations in the world had to be preferable to the prospect of spending the foreseeable future at the mercy of James Naylor and his cronies. But the phone would also mean tackling the stairs, for there seemed little likelihood of there being an extension in the cellars.

And then, as she heard the first sounds of approaching heels in the corridor beyond the door, Lianne knew exactly what she had to do. She closed her eyes, took a deep breath, and tensed herself in readiness.

She saw the door handle turn and watched as if through a smoked glass screen as the heavy oak swung inwards, the whole scene seemingly in slow motion. Paul came into view, arms cuffed behind his back, the leash from his collar trailing backwards and held loosely by Marika as she followed him into the room. She saw the white booted legs protruding from behind the bed and stopped short, momentarily off balance. Lianne seized her chance. Lunging forward she swung her forearm hard, cutting a horizontal semi-circle, and her steel-clad wrist and hand drove into Marika's kidneys.

The dusky dominatrix let out a grunt of surprise and then cried out as Lianne twisted and swung her other arm, burying flesh and steel into the girl's midriff. Marika tried to take a step towards her. She dropped the leash and reached out, but the delayed reaction of the second blow, which had landed full in her solar plexus, brought her up short. With a strangled gasp her knees buckled and she fell forward, hands clutching at her chest. Without hesitation Lianne launched herself, and a combined weight of flesh and metal crashed down onto the girl's back and shoved her against the hard stone.

Lianne rolled over and looked up at Paul. He was standing open-mouthed in the middle of the room, looking from Christina's unconscious form, to Lianne and Marika, and back again. Beneath Lianne Marika was making a half-hearted attempt to struggle free, but the double blow, combined with the impact of Lianne and the wall had knocked the fight out of her – if only temporarily.

'Don't just stand there!' Lianne screamed at Paul. 'Get the key – on the bed there!' Paul appeared to come back to life, his head jerking from side to side. 'It's there – on the bed!' Lianne urged him. 'You should be able to get your cuffs off.'

It seemed to take him an eternity, working blind behind his back, but eventually Paul managed to get the key into one of the padlocks and turn it. It then took several more seconds before he was able to twist the lock free and pull the leather manacle from his wrist. The second lock yielded much more easily.

'Bring them here,' Lianne snapped. 'Get her arms and put them on her. Quickly! She's starting to struggle again.'

For Marika it was too late. Against two adversaries, even though one of them was severely restricted in her movements, it was a hopeless contest. A few minutes later, cuffed and gagged, her ankles and knees bound together with leather leashes, she lay on the bed glaring at the two of them as Paul hauled Lianne upright and then unlocked the chains that hobbled his ankles. He tossed the manacles onto the bed alongside Marika and stared at Christina.

'How the hell did you manage that?' he asked, still trying to get his own breath back. Lianne grinned and clicked her booted feet together.

'Just call me Hammer Toes,' she said. 'Plus the fact that she ought to make sure doors are properly open before she tries to walk through them. Is she still breathing?'

Paul knelt down and examined the unconscious amazon. 'Yeah, she's still with us,' he confirmed. 'But we need to get away from this place fast. Come here and let me get you out of that lot.' Lianne shook her head.

'No chance,' she said. 'That key doesn't fit any of these locks and I don't know where the proper key is. You'll have to help me up the stairs.'

'We'll never make it,' Paul said. 'They'll be in the lounge now and the windows look out on the main driveway. From what I've seen we'd have to walk right by them to get to the garage where they keep the cars. The only other way is to go through the barn and out around the back of it, but there's still a chance we'd be seen crossing the yard. The end window of the lounge overlooks that area.'

'Then you'll have to make a break on your own,' Lianne said. 'I can't move very fast in this lot, but you can, especially if you take those boots off.'

'No, I'm not leaving you behind,' Paul insisted. 'There must be another way.'

'There is,' Lianne announced suddenly. She pointed down at Christina. 'Get her outfit off her.' Paul stared at her uncomprehending. 'Get her stuff off her,' Lianne repeated. 'She's a bit taller than you are, but it should fit near enough. And if you wear her mask as well, from a distance anyone would think you *were* her. And if anyone looks out of the lounge and sees Christina leading me on a chain they'll just assume the vicious bitch is taking me back to the barn for a bit of extra entertainment.'

'It'll never work!' Paul exclaimed, but he bent down and began turning the blonde onto her stomach, revealing the back lacing which fastened the leather leotard.

'Just do it,' Lianne urged. 'It'll be getting dark up there by now in any case, so they won't get a clear view. Hurry up, before someone starts wondering what's happened to these two.'

'I shouldn't worry too much about that,' Paul said, working furiously on the laces. 'Marika made some crack about amusing herself with me before supper. The cow reckoned she needed to work up an appetite. They'd already assumed this one was having fun at your expense.'

'We still can't afford to waste time,' Lianne said. 'And I'm not going to be much help to you, not with these things on my hands.'

The next twenty minutes were the longest of Lianne's life. It seemed to take Paul forever to strip Christina and then, as he was just about to remove his own costume, he had to stop and cuff the big woman as she began to show signs of returning consciousness. Lianne stopped him gagging her as well, worried she might choke.

'Keep the gag handy for when she comes round,

though,' she said. 'I should think these rooms are fairly soundproof, but there's no point in taking chances.'

It seemed strange seeing Paul completely naked and without the wig, but still in full makeup. He seemed embarrassed by his nudity and only too eager to hide it inside the white leather. Lianne had to help with the back lacing, her fingers awkward as she wound the thongs in and out of the ski hook fastenings, and Paul had to reach around and knot them himself.

As Lianne had predicted, the outfit was slightly loose on him, though not as much as she had feared. The boots were a perfect fit however, and the mask had adjustable lacing at the back to ensure a snug embrace. The gloves, which Christina had put on after fitting Lianne into the steel clothing, also had laces, and by the time they had finished Lianne was confident that anyone seeing Paul from a distance would indeed be fooled.

Christina was still only semi-conscious and groaning with the pain from her leg, so Paul contented himself with locking a collar about her neck and connecting it to the bed with a short length of chain. Lianne was eager to get going, but he had one task left and it was obviously borne of a need to seek revenge. From the rack on the wall he selected the largest dildo from the extensive range and took it across to Marika. He untied her legs, pulled them apart, and then wound the leashes around her ankles and tied the ends to the legs of the bed. He then quickly unclipped the gusset panel in her leotard and peeled it back, revealing her dark bush and pink labia. Marika stared up at him and began to shake her head.

'It's no good protesting,' Paul said calmly. 'You were only too willing to use one of these on me upstairs. Now it's your turn.' He prised her sex lips apart and inserted the tip of the phallus, rotating it back and forth to assist its entry. 'I guess it does us all good to be on the receiving end once in a while.' He thrust the large shaft home in one smooth movement. From behind her gag Marika squealed, but Paul ignored her and refastened the crotch panel to keep the rubber cock in place.

'Be grateful I haven't got time to put one up the back as well,' Paul told her as he straightened up. He turned to Lianne and put his arms around her shoulders. 'Come on then,' he said, 'let's get out of here.'

Paul solved the problem of the stairs by carrying Lianne. He was much stronger than she had suspected, and they reached the ground floor with him barely out of breath.

It was dusk when they emerged into the yard, the lights from the lounge window burning brightly through the open curtains. Lianne risked a quick glance to her left and saw the outline of two figures inside the room, but if they saw the pair of them, they gave no indication that they suspected anything was amiss. Nevertheless, every shuffling step seemed an eternity and, when they finally reached the sanctuary of the barn, Lianne was close to a nervous collapse.

As they passed by the semi-circle of chairs Paul made a cursory search, but there was no sign of the key that would unlock Lianne's bondage, and no time to waste in looking any further.

'We'll just have to go as we are,' he said. 'If we make it we'll have to cut you out of that lot.'

The garage was unlocked and so were all the vehicles in it; two large saloons, a sports car, the van in which Lianne had originally arrived, and a larger van. Paul quickly checked them all. There were keys in the ignition of the sports car, in one of the saloons, and in the larger van.

'We'll take the van,' he decided. 'You'll never be able to fit into any of the others properly.' Fitting into even the chosen van was no easy matter, even with the passenger seat pushed right back. But with Paul's assistance Lianne finally made it, her legs straight out in front of her, her back pressed upright against the upholstery of the seat. Paul fastened the safety belt across her chest, patted her thigh, and closed the door. He then ran around to climb behind the wheel.

'Haven't you forgotten something?' Lianne asked, nodding towards the garage doors which were still firmly closed. Paul reached over and picked up a small black device from on top of the dashboard. It was about the size of a television remote control, though it only had two buttons – one red and one green. He wound down his window, pointed the device towards the doors, and pressed the green button. Neither of them could detect the remote eye, but he simply waved the box around until, with a loud clunk, the electric motor started up and the door nearest to them began to rise.

'So far, so good,' he muttered, tossing the control unit back onto the dash and reaching for the ignition key. 'Let's just hope this baby starts.' He turned the key, the starter whirred, and the engine roared into life. Paul looked across at Lianne and grinned. 'Hold tight, my little tin can baby,' he shouted and eased the gear lever into first. 'This is gonna be hairy!'

CHAPTER TWENTY-FIVE

Upon their eventual return to Nadia's house, Paul and Lianne were greeted like long lost children. Ellen clung onto Lianne, sobbing and laughing at the same time, whilst Nadia herself found Paul's new outfit much to her liking.

'I quite like that myself,' she said. 'With a few small alterations it should fit me just fine.'

Paul looked from her to Lianne. 'I'll have a new one made for you especially,' he promised. 'But I think we'd like to hang on to this one – as a souvenir.'

Nadia smiled, but said nothing. She had known Paul for too long to be fooled. She turned to Lianne instead.

'And as for you, young lady,' she said, 'anyone would think you were auditioning for *The Wizard of Oz*. I shouldn't go out in the rain in that, if I were you!' Everyone laughed, including Lianne. 'Mind you,' Nadia continued, 'it's a really stunning concept. This Christina woman certainly has an inventive brain.'

'Maybe,' Lianne agreed, 'but I'd like to get out of it now, if you don't mind.'

Paul stroked her cheek. 'Listen,' he said, 'I've been thinking on the way back. Yes, we could probably hack off the catches, but it'd vandalise a superb piece of workmanship. On the other hand, I know a discreet locksmith who could make a duplicate key for that in about ten minutes flat.'

'Only he's not here now, is he?' Lianne pointed out.

'And I don't fancy the prospect of spending the entire night in this sardine can. I can't even use the loo.'

'We'll compromise then,' Paul suggested. 'I'll cut through the catch that holds that part in place. We can easily have that repaired afterwards.'

'That's easy enough for you to suggest,' Lianne said. 'You're not the one wearing this lot. I feel like I've got my legs stuck in drainpipes and sacks of coal tied to my feet.'

'I'll make it well worth your while,' Paul promised. 'I'm sure we can think of something to keep your mind occupied until the locksmith gets here in the morning.'

'I'm sure we can,' Lianne agreed, 'but it's still no dice. I've been locked in this contraption for what seems like the best part of a lifetime – or the worst part, to be more accurate – and right now I want nothing more than to have a nice long soak in a hot bath.' Paul looked disappointed. 'But,' Lianne continued, 'get this thing off me, and when it's been repaired I'll wear it for you as a special treat – though there will be a few conditions.'

'What sort of conditions?' Paul asked warily.

Lianne grinned. 'Come here a minute,' she said.

With a puzzled expression Paul leaned close and Lianne whispered something to him. The others saw his eyes widen as she spoke, but could not hear what was being proposed. 'It's up to you,' she finally said aloud, giving him a seductive smile.

Paul stroked his chin with one leather-gloved hand, but quickly nodded. 'Okay,' he said. 'It's a deal.'

'What's a deal?' Nadia asked.

Lianne's smile broadened. 'That's between Paul and me,' she smirked. 'But I'll need a rubber maid's outfit.'

'Are you sure you want me here?' Ellen asked, adjusting the last suspender that held her sheer stockings to the leather corset. 'I can go if you like. There're beds made up in several of the other rooms.'

'I wouldn't hear of it,' Lianne said. She picked up the piece of curved steel that had earlier been covering her sex and bottom, and turned it over and over in her hands. 'If it hadn't been for you I wouldn't have known about any of this. No, you can share the fun with me tonight, and tomorrow night you can share my new maid with me.'

'I can't believe he agreed so easily,' said Ellen.

'Can't you? I can. Paul absolutely adores dressing up – especially as a girl. He used the suit thing as an excuse – just a bit of a laugh. As far as anyone else was concerned it was just an initiation routine, used on all the new girls. Naylor saw through that, though. The only thing he didn't appreciate was that forcing Paul to dress up as a woman and then tying or chaining him up was exactly what the poor dear's been craving for all his life.

'Even this is a good get out for him. He can pretend he's only doing it so I agree to wear the tin outfit again.' She nodded towards the discarded metal bondage suit. 'But I know the truth. And what's more, he knows I know it.'

'So what are you going to do tonight?' Ellen asked, stepping into the tiny leather triangle that was her panties. Lianne smiled.

'Just about anything that takes my fancy… or yours.' Her eyes sparkled mischievously. 'First of all I'm going to spend a good hour in a deep hot bath, so if Paul gets up here before I'm ready, you'll just have to make a start without me.'

CHAPTER TWENTY-SIX

'I suppose we might as well put everything on hold for the moment,' Simon Prescott said, somewhat dejectedly. The two of them were sitting alone now, a large decanter on the coffee table between them. Nadia's eyebrows knitted together and she reached for her brandy glass.

'Why do you say that?' she asked. Simon was idly thumbing through a pile of glossy prints, the results of the final shoot before Paul and Lianne had been abducted.

'Well, with no artist, we'll just be piling up a backlog, won't we?' he replied. Nadia sipped, delicately.

'The Jimmy Naylor's of this world are not so bloody rare as they might like to think themselves,' she said. She leaned over and took a large manila envelope from the magazine shelf below the coffee table. 'You might like to take a look at some of these,' she suggested. Simon looked up from his photographs and stared at the envelope. 'Go on, take it,' Nadia urged. 'It won't bite you.'

Laying aside his prints, Simon stretched across and took the envelope. It was unsealed and quite bulky. Slowly he drew out its contents, a half inch thick folio of A4 sheets, the uppermost of which was pale blue card and blank. Carefully, he drew it aside.

'Take your time,' Nadia said very quietly. 'And then tell me what you think.'

'I can tell you that now,' Simon replied. 'If the rest are as good as this top one, the man's a genius!'

'Who said it was a man?' Nadia retorted. Simon whistled.

'These were done by a woman?' he asked incredulously. He stared down at the first two pictures, which he was holding side by side. They both depicted women – no, he saw, the same woman in each case – dressed as erotically as anything Paul and Nadia had ever managed to create. In the first drawing she was wearing an outfit that consisted primarily of leather straps, which concealed far less than they enhanced. Rings set in these straps were attached to ropes from which the girl was suspended like some bizarre puppet, leaning forward at an angle of about forty-five degrees. Her arms and legs were spread wide, and a penis gag distorting her otherwise beautiful features.

In the second illustration she was wearing a more conventional rubber catsuit, complete with an all-in-one hood which covered her hair, but which left her features framed and exposed. On her feet she wore lockable ankle boots, with heels that were easily six inches high. She was standing in a straddled position, about to lower herself onto a rubber dildo which projected up from a knee high stool towards her sex, which was clearly visible thanks to the strategic cutout in the crotch of the suit. The quality of the penmanship was unbelievable; the light reflecting and dancing off every ripple and distortion in the rubber, and the sense of anticipation on the girl's face a wonder to behold.

'Her name's Sonia Hughes,' Nadia said. 'She's Welsh, but she's just graduated down on the south coast with a double first. I've had these for several weeks, actually.'

'Then why didn't you show us before?' Simon demanded. 'She's even better than Naylor.'

'I know,' Nadia sighed, 'but at the time we had our team, didn't we? And I happen to believe in loyalty.'

'So, all the time Naylor was plotting to rip us off, you were looking after his interests?' Simon said. 'Bloody ironic, isn't it?'

'Yes, it is,' Nadia confessed. 'But at least everything's turned out okay in the end and poor old Jimmy's lost everything. Thanks to Ellen's quick thinking we still have all your photographs and all his original artwork. I don't think he'll be suing us for them back, do you?'

'I wouldn't put anything past him,' Simon growled. 'I reckon we should call the police and tell them what happened. What they did to Paul and Lianne, they could do to someone else.'

'No police,' Nadia said firmly. 'I know we're not doing anything illegal here, but the publicity could be ruinous. We'd have every oddball thrill seeker climbing the fences and hiding around with long lens cameras. We'd have to move from here and start up all over again somewhere else, and I don't have the money for that — not yet, anyway.'

'But we can't just let them get away with it!' Simon protested.

'I agree,' Nadia said. 'And we won't. I've got a few little surprises lined up for Mr James Naylor, I can promise you. But there's no rush. From what Paul and Lianne said, the big blonde dyke has got a broken leg and, as she seems to be a central part of their operation, it'll be several weeks before they're in a position to make their next move. Meanwhile, I'll put a discreet private investigator onto keeping a watch on their place.'

'And business as usual here?' Simon suggested, hopefully.

Nadia nodded. 'Yes. We'll all take a couple of days off, to give Paul and Nadia a chance to get over their adventures, and I'll give Sonia a call and arrange for her to join us.'

'What's she like, this Sonia?' Simon asked. He was looking at the third picture now and the same girl was trussed in a hog-tie, her arms bound behind her back and her ankles drawn up to meet her wrists. Her hair, which was long and dark, had been braided with leather thongs and these in turn had been attached to the wrist and ankle chains, forcing her head cruelly back. From the expression on her face, however, she was not as distressed as she was excited.

'You're looking at her,' Nadia said calmly. Simon's eyes opened wide and he stared at the drawings anew.

'You mean this is her?' he squawked.

'In the flesh,' Nadia confirmed. 'Or should I say, flesh and rubber? Quite lovely, isn't she?'

'Are you telling me that this gorgeous piece poses for her own bondage pictures?'

'Yes. Apparently there's a little club of arty types at her University that are well into it. Don't forget – rubber, PVC, and bondage paraphernalia are all very hip these days.'

'Well, I'll be buggered!' Simon whistled. 'And does she intend doing the same thing here?'

'Part of the deal,' Nadia said. 'She's very keen. I had thought of getting her in anyway, even if we didn't use her artistic skills, but now she can have the best of both worlds. And so can we,' she added.

'That won't affect Lianne, will it?' Simon said, his

brow furrowing. 'I mean, I know she's the newest recruit, but it hardly seems fair, not after all she's been through. And she did help Paul escape. If it hadn't been for her Naylor would still have him prisoner.'

'Lianne will be staying,' Nadia assured him. 'Assuming she still wants to stay, that is.'

'Oh, I think she does,' Simon chuckled. 'I must admit, that first session, I thought she'd be off like a shot afterwards. But she's tougher than she looks.'

'Not only tough,' Nadia said. 'Like a lot of people, she's found out something about her hidden depths. Ellen was very perceptive with her, you know.'

'And she's been pretty perceptive in Paul's case, you know. I nearly fell over when he got out of the motor looking like that. I almost didn't recognise him.'

'I think there might be a little flame kindling between those two, actually,' Nadia laughed. 'Young Lianne's figured Paul out quicker than any of you lot did. You thought those antics of his in that cat woman suit were just down to his warped sense of humour, didn't you?'

'But you knew differently, I suppose?' Simon grinned. Nadia smiled.

'I've seen a lot of things in my lifetime,' she said. 'And hopefully, I shall see a lot more.'

'I'll drink to that,' Simon retorted, and looked about for his glass.

CHAPTER TWENTY-SEVEN

Paul was visibly surprised when he entered the bedroom to be confronted by Ellen clad in her gleaming dominatrix outfit. He looked about, taking in the tangle of metal in the corner and the array of straps on the bed and pulled the silk robe closer about himself.

'Where's Lianne?' he asked, his voice too hoarse to be natural. Ellen nodded in the direction of the bathroom door.

'She's having a nice long soak,' she said.

Paul looked even more confused. 'So what are you doing here?'

'I'm the warm-up act,' Ellen cooed. She stood with her legs slightly apart and her gloved hands on her hips. Paul looked her up and down, his eyes riveted finally on the long boots, with their towering heels. They made her as tall as him, and he felt strangely uneasy about that. Had it been Lianne standing before him he would have been surer of his position, but Ellen was a different kettle of fish. She was quirky in an entirely unpredictable way, for she had a devilish sense of humour and you never knew what she might think up next. Paul shuffled his bare feet uncomfortably.

'What are you going to do?' he asked.

Ellen stepped forward and grasped his robe. 'I'm going to get you naked, for a start,' she breathed sexily. She tugged at the belt and it fell away and a moment later the entire garment slid to the floor about his ankles. She turned to the bed and picked up a pair of leather manacles, connected by a single steel link.

'Turn around,' she ordered. Paul hesitated. 'Just do as you're told,' she said. 'It's only for a little while; so you can't interfere with what I'm going to do.'

'That's what worries me,' said Paul. 'Just exactly what *are* you going to do?'

Ellen winked. 'Well, that would be telling. Now, are we going to do this right, or shall I just tell Lianne that you're acting like a big baby and the whole deal's off? I'm not going to stand around all night you know, and Lianne expects you to be ready for her by the time she comes back.'

With a sigh of resignation Paul slowly turned his back to her and she drew his arms behind him. The cuffs went about his wrists one at a time and he heard the click as she fastened the two small padlocks. He felt an exciting little shiver of trepidation as he realised it was too late to argue any more. He had been made helpless over the past few days in genuinely threatening circumstances, but somehow submitting himself to a woman he knew was far worse. She grasped his shoulders and turned him around again. Paul tried to act nonchalantly.

'Now what, dear mistress?'

The slap across his face was not that hard, but the impact of her open palm was sufficient to make him reel backwards, his heels catching in the hem of his robe so that he toppled off balance. Luckily, the end of the bed saved him from any serious damage and he lay on the mattress, gasping more with indignant surprise than pain.

'You've forgotten the rules of the game,' Ellen chided

him. 'So watch that tongue, or I'll take a strap to your backside. Now, sit up and try to behave yourself.'

By the time Paul had struggled into a sitting position Ellen had already selected a pair of ankle cuffs and bent quickly to fasten them into position. He peered down as she worked, noting the few inches of chain between them.

'Now,' she said, standing up again, 'I think we'll have a collar and a cock and ball strap.' She fitted the collar first; a broad band of stiff leather which forced Paul to hold his chin well up, and then made him stand again for the final accoutrement. He winced as the narrow leather band was tightened behind his scrotum and then the second strap drawn about the base of his penis, though the touch of her gloved fingers was already causing it to swell.

'That will do nicely,' Ellen said, stepping back. She turned and picked up a long switch and pointed the tip of it towards his genitalia. He winced again and tried to retreat, but the footboard was right behind him. Slowly, Ellen brought up the braided leather until it was just brushing his pendulous balls and began to work it back and forth. Within seconds his erection was complete, his cock bulging through the restraining ring of leather, and his breath was coming in shorter and shorter gasps. Ellen smiled.

'That's not going to last very long, now is it?' she teased. 'You seem to be just a little overexcited – and I can't have you disappointing Lianne.' She cast the switch aside and dropped to her knees in front of him. In one cool palm she cupped his heavy testicles, and in the other she gripped his throbbing shaft. Her head bobbed forward and he felt the wet warmth of her mouth engulfed him. Her lips, tongue, and hands worked with great expertise and Paul groaned loudly, straining to resist the tide that was surging upwards through his loins – but to no avail.

With a long, drawn-out moan he came in her, his seed spurting in agonising jolts as it forced its way past the twin restrictions. His knees buckled as the strength fled from his legs. Ellen was unrelenting, her lips working furiously as she sucked him completely dry.

'Those Arab straps aren't all they're cracked up to be,' she said at last, rising elegantly and seductively licking her lips. 'They're supposed to inhibit the male climax.'

'I – I'm sorry,' Paul blurted. 'I just couldn't help myself.'

'So I noticed.' Ellen smiled and reached out to caress the tip of his already dwindling phallus. 'Still, I reckon you'll last a good bit longer next time.'

When Lianne finally entered the bedroom she stood for several seconds studying the tableau. Ellen was lounging back in the easy chair, her long booted legs crossed, a switch dangling idly from the fingers of her right hand. Paul was kneeling back on his haunches in the middle of the carpet, his hands bound behind him, and his head held erect by the collar about his throat. His cock reared from his dark groin, the veins clearly visible beneath the taut flesh, and the black leather of the two straps digging deeply into him.

She turned to Ellen. 'Have you—?'

Ellen smiled like the cat that knows it has her prey cornered. 'Let's just say he's nice and ready for you.'

'So I see,' Lianne replied softly. 'Can we have the cuffs off him now?'

She moved slowly to Paul and stood in front of him as Ellen released his wrists. Her long lacy robe hung open at the front and she could feel his eyes burning into her body.

'I thought this would make a change from all the rubber and leather,' she purred – and indeed it did. She was still corseted, but the sexy garment was fashioned from satin and lace, as was the tiny triangle which covered her sex. She wore gloves too, but again these were satin, as were the dainty high-heeled mules on her feet. Her legs she had left bare, the lightly tanned flesh as smooth as the finest silk.

'Stand up,' she said, once Ellen had removed the final shackle. Paul stiffly rose to his feet and stood uncertainly in front of her. Lianne reached out and took a light hold about his waist, keeping him at arm's length. 'It's up to you now,' she breathed. Behind her she heard the soft clink of chains and was aware of an even softer click as the door closed behind Ellen. She continued to stare into Paul's eyes.

'What do you want me to do?' he whispered.

'I want you to act like any red-blooded male,' she goaded. 'That's assuming you can, of course.'

By way of reply, he suddenly scooped her up into his arms, turned, and lowered her onto the bed.

'Is this what you want?' he rasped, his fingers exploring between her thighs, insinuating themselves inside the thin material which covered her lips there. Lianne closed her eyes and nodded.

'Yes,' she urged him hoarsely. 'For tonight I'm yours to do with exactly as you please. But after tonight you're going to be all mine.' She opened her eyes and looked up at him. 'You do understand that, don't you?'

'Yes, I understand that,' he said, but he was already easing himself over her, his knees forcing her thighs wider. Lianne slipped a hand down and released one of the ties that secured her little G-string. Taking her cue, Paul gently tugged the other side loose and drew the tiny garment from beneath her bottom. She followed his unspoken demand and lifted her hips slightly to help him. Her fingers sought and found his bulging member, but he slid away from her, crouched between her soft thighs, and buried his face against her perfumed flesh, his mouth closing on her with unerring accuracy.

She gasped as his tongue probed between her labia, finding her clitoris immediately and setting off the little sparks of current that she was coming to know so well. Her back arched and her fingers roamed to her own nipples, pulling and twisting them and adding an exquisite sensation of pain to the floods of pleasure which were washing throughout her body.

'Oh yes…!' she wailed. 'Oh yesss…!' Her hands flew to his head. She grasped his hair and pulled him up. 'Please!' she begged him. '*Please…*!'

Paul eased forward and she desperately gripped his bursting erection once more. She steered the swollen knob towards its target and gasped with delight as it instantly pushed its way inside her.

'The strap!' he suddenly groaned, but Lianne shook her head wildly.

'Forget it!' she gasped. 'Please, don't stop!'

Paul could wait no longer himself. He thrust into her until the rough edge of the cock strap was pressing against her mound. Lianne heard a far-off voice wailing like a banshee. As Paul began to move slowly the wail descended into a long, animal-like groan of sated pleasure and Lianne exploded into the first of many blissful orgasms...

It was going to be a long night.

It was also, she hoped, going to be a very long life.

For both of them.

Together.

Already available from Chimera:

Coming soon from Chimera:

All the above are/will be available at your local bookshop or newsagent, or by post or telephone from: B.B.C.S., P.O. Box 941, Hull, HU1 3VQ. **(24 hour Telephone Credit Card Line: 01482 224626)**.

To order, send: Title, author, ISBN number and price for each book ordered, your full name and address, cheque or postal order payable to B.B.C.S. for the total amount, and allow the following for postage and packing:

UK and BFPO: £1.00 for the first book, and 50p for each additional book to a maximum of £3.50.

Overseas and Eire: £2.00 for the first book, £1.00 for the second and 50p for each additional book.

All titles £4.99 (US$7.95)